回憶的沙漏

中 英 對 照 詩 集

Sandglass of Memory

Poetry Collection (Chinese & English)

林明理 著　　吳 鈞 譯
Writer: Lin Mimgli　　Translator: Wu Jun

插上外語的翅膀

讓詩飛向世界

賀林明理中英文對照
詩集出版

山東大學吳開晉
辛卯之冬

林明理畫作《林中飛瀑》，刊登《人間福報》2011.10.25

林明理畫作《秋景》，刊登《人間福報》2011.5.30

2010.08.17吳鈞教授在悉尼大學

2010.10.07吳鈞教授在悉尼大學做報告

2011.11.03吳鈞於新南威爾士大學報告

吳鈞與開晉叔父在會議室

2009.08.09吳鈞與開晉叔父攝影於家中

山東省全國中文核心期刊《時代文學》封面特別推薦林明理的詩、散文、評論

2011年古遠清教授來訪台北教育大學研討會合照

序

中南財經政法大學世界華文文學研究所所長
古遠清教授

　　我帶著驚異的眼光讀林明理的《回憶的沙漏——中英對照詩集》。

　　我驚異的第一個原因是林明理的個人氣質曾給我留下難忘的印象。記得2010年在阿里山初次見面時，同行的深圳文友說她打扮得像一位日本姑娘，一點都不像中年人。她氣質優雅，就似在人們休閑的地方出現的岸畔之樹。她給人的印象是杉林溪的風，是帶著清涼鈴鐺的流螢，是閃爍於萬巒峰頂的千燈。

　　我驚異的還有一個深層的原因：林明理在大學裡教過「憲法」及「國父思想」等課程，以為在她詩中一定會留下其政教的痕跡。她一定會意氣風發，慷慨高歌大寫那些關懷社會、抨擊時弊的題材，可翻遍《回憶的沙漏──中英對照詩集》，均找不到這樣的政治詩，找不到她當年為《民眾日報》等報刊寫評論時為民請命亂石崩雲般勁健奔放、磅礴有力的氣魄，而有的是〈夏荷〉、〈雨夜〉、〈流星雨〉、〈拂曉之前〉、〈秋暮〉、〈牧羊女的晚禱〉、〈早霧〉這類如雲，如霧，如幽林曲澗，如珠玉之輝的低迴婉轉之作。在她詩裡，人們聽到的是樹與星群齊舞的足音，所看到的是急緩地往雲裡行和在煙波細雨中南飛的大雁。

　　我驚異的第三個原因是林明理每首詩均很短。她決不和別人比「長城氣勢」，看誰寫得長。其作品所選取的多是一朵感情的浪花，一點飄渺的思緒，一個生活的鏡頭。但短小並不完全是從形體著眼──諸如句短、段少、字少之類。因為短小不只是指它的形式，同時也是指它的內容。小詩作者在處理題材時，必須使內容集中概括，形體凝聚。既短小而要寓意高度濃縮，使意象豐厚鮮活，這就要求作者有精巧的構思，要讓它的內容帶一點跳躍性，句與句之間有較大的彈性與張力。試讀林明理的〈回憶的沙漏〉的下半段：

......

大地上一切已從夢中醒覺

山影終將無法藏匿

我卻信，我將孤獨痛苦地

漫行於沙漠世界

夜，依然濃重

徜徉於

白堤的浮萍之間

　　這裡寫的是一刹那的意境，無疑有不可明言的「孤獨
痛苦」的內容，可作者並沒有將「濃重的夜色」和盤托
出，其中「漫行於沙漠世界」所抒發的人生體驗，具有不
使人動情卻令人思索的特色。

　　關於小詩，一直有種種誤讀，如有人認為隨意捕捉幾
個意象便可敷衍成篇。其實，小詩要寫好，不在構思上下
一番苦功，是無法打動讀者的。林明理的經驗證明，要寫
好小詩必須有清俊、秀逸、雋永的風格。

　　以海洋為師，以星月為友，以書籍為伴的林明理，她
寫詩所追求的正是清新俏麗，含蓄雋永。這裡不妨再舉一
首她寫的〈雨後的夜晚〉；

　　　雪松寂寂
　　　風裹我
　　　聲音在輕喚著沉睡的星群
　　　梧桐也悄然若思

　　　路盡處，燈火迷茫
　　　霧中
　　　一個孤獨的身影
　　　靜聽蟲鳴

　　作者在這裡用婉轉的歌喉、纏綿的情調譜出了一首
「悄然若思」的衷曲。讀林明理這類娟美而富於生活情趣
的小詩，就好似繁星滿空的夜晚推開小窗，習習涼風飄了
進來；又好似一彎潺潺的細流，緩緩地流進讀者的心田。
林明理從學校提前退休後沒有生活在「藍」「綠」爭鬥的

漩渦中心，與現實鬥爭相距較遠，但由於她的小詩處處顯示著女性的細膩、溫婉的特徵，風格含蓄典雅，清麗雋永，故仍為不同營壘的讀者所鍾愛。

　　林明理是近年崛起的詩壇新人。她成長於一個獨特的環境，那是臺灣著名詩社「創世紀」的誕生地左營。那裡海浪翻騰，地處偏遠。南部詩人在這裡生生息息：從張默到林明理，形成了一種獨異的左營人文景觀。

　　末了，我衷心祝明理在秋日的港灣裡譜出更多的「北浦夜歌」；在行經木棧道時，在蟲鳥細鳴的陽光裡，「只對老街、小巷，為明天擁抱天空！」

2011年11月5日

譯者的話

　　最初認識臺灣詩人林明理女士是通過我的叔父吳開晉教授介紹的。記得去年的年初，接到叔父轉來的電子郵件，裡面附有林明理的幾首詩歌，叔父囑我幫著翻譯一下。從那以後，就經常讀到明理的詩歌了。

　　讀林明理的詩歌，感到她的詩歌就像她的人一樣熱情清純，又精緻靈巧。讀她的詩歌，眼前就會出現一幅幅青翠朦朧的山水畫，在她的筆下，大自然的一草一木都靈動可愛，山光湖色都蘊涵寓意。她的詩歌中意象豐富，千變萬化。例如她的詩歌中有叼走晨星的小畫眉鳥，有酣睡著的常青藤種子，還有散滿霜風的弓箭和山芙蓉的低吟，掠過細石的小溪……。讀明理的詩歌，就像是漫步於大自然的廣闊天地，行走在萬千意象的叢林之中。

A Few Words From The Translator

The first time when I heard about Ms. Lin Mingli is from the e-mail of my uncle, Professor Wu Kaijin. I remember it was early in the year 2010, my uncle gave me the e-mail and included several pieces of poems of Lin Mingli. He asked me to help her for the translation. From then on, I often read her poems.

When I read the poems of Lin Minli, I always feel the passion and pureness of them which are full of delicacy and dexterity. Her poems are just like her personality. When I read her poems, I seemed to see in front of me the paintings of the landscape with green river and hazy mountains. In her poems, the grass and trees of the nature are all vivid and lovely. The description of the natural view is with deep symbolic implications. There are varieties of images and rich and colorful descriptions in her poems. Such as the wood thrush

　　應明理的邀請，選譯了她的詩歌六十六首。翻譯她的詩歌的過程，也是欣賞她描繪的山光湖色的過程，更是體驗一位執著的詩人在藝術道路上攀登的過程。

　　在明理的第一本漢英雙語詩集出版之際，我誠摯地祝願她在詩歌藝術的道路上不斷進取開拓，寫出更多更美的詩歌。正如她在一首詩歌中寫的：「正似探訪的螢火蟲，等待逸出……」。

吳鈞

2011年11月5日

picking up the last star at dawn, the seeds of the evergreen having sound sleep,and also the bow covered through with snow and frost,the mountain lotus 'crooning,the fleeting brook———. To read Lin Mingli's poems is just like to ramble about the extensive fields of the nature, to walk through the forest of myriad of images.

With the invitation of Lin Minli, I have chosen and translated sixty-six of her poems and collected them into this poetry anthology. The process of my translation of her poems is the enjoyment of the landscape in her writing, and also the process of feeling her clambering towards the literary peaks.

Here I express my best wishes for the publication of her first Chinese-English poetry anthology. Wish her more and better poems in the future and continuously move forward on the road of artistic pursuits. It is just like the writing in her poem: "As if an exploring firefly,waiting for surpassing———".

Wu Jun

Nov.5,2011

目次

Contents

霧

在故鄉紅石崗的坡上

牽出了

我家老山羊匿在銀月裡玩

夢見了

那是辣子，或是包穀

門檻還有許多菜香

阿公背我

為我淌汗

而我滿心歡喜

因為金星星繡滿了我紅搖籃

2009.12.24作

臺灣《乾坤》詩刊2010.04夏季號第54期

Fog

On the slope of red rocky hillock

I pulled out

our old goat hidden in the silver moon playing

In my dream I saw

Capsicum,or corn

With fragrant vegetables by the door

My grandpa,carried me on his back

Sweating for me

I was only fascinated

In the golden stars stitching on my red cradle

刊美國 *Poems of the World*，2011秋季號

想念的季節

飛吧，
三月的木棉，
哭紅了春天的眼睛。

飛吧，
風箏載著同一張笑臉，
心卻緊緊抓住了線。

飛吧，
楓葉輕落溪底，
行腳已沒有風塵。

飛吧，
我們都把心門打開，
讓光明的窗照射進來。

The Season OF Yearning

Flying,

The ceiba of March,

In spring you cry your eyes red.

Flying,

The kite carried the same smiling face,

The heart yet grasped the thread tight.

Flying,

Maple leaves gently down the bottom of the brook,

Pettitoes were traceless.

Flying

We all open the doors of our hearts

Let in the bright light

飛吧，

螢火蟲，

藏進滿天星，我是

沉默的夜。

2008.11.12作
新疆期刊獎獲獎期刊《綠風》詩刊，總第183期，2009.第
3期；臺灣《人間福報》2010.3.31刊登詩畫

Flying,

Firebug,

Hiding in the stars of the sky,I am

The silent night.

刊美國 *Poems of the World*，2011秋季號

樹林入口

時間是水塘交替的光影

它的沉默浸滿了我的瞳仁

雨沖出凹陷的泥地

在承接暗藍的蒼穹

一隻小彎嘴畫眉

正叼走最後一顆晨星

呵四季從不懂謊言

就像我的心啊

披滿十一月秋天

除了想你已無處躲藏

當太陽掠過樺樹上端

The Entrance Of The Forest

Time is the alternated light shadow of the pool

It silently soaked through my pupils

The rain water rushed out the muddy cupped land

To meet the far reaches of the dark blue horizon

A little throstle with crooked beak

Is picking away the last star at dawn

Oh,the seasons will never tell the lie

It just like my heart

Is filled with the odor of autumn in October

Nowhere to hide except to miss you

When the sun swept past the top of the birch

索性把思念變成一條小溪
讓重疊的濃綠時時潺潺鳴響

2009.09.14作
原載台灣《創世紀》詩雜誌，第161期，2009.12月冬季號；
轉載山東省作協主辦《新世紀文學選刊》2010.03

Willfully I turn the missing into the brook

Let the overlapped dark green echo the rill all the time

曾經

你輕俏得似掠過細石的
小溪，似水塘底白霧，揉縮
隨我步向籬柵探尋你的澄碧
我卻驟然顛覆了時空
熟悉你的每一次巧合

你微笑像幅半完成的畫
淨潔是你的幾筆刻劃，無羈無求
那青松的頌讚，風的吟游：
誰能於萬籟之中盈盈閃動？每當
黃昏靠近窗口

Once

You are brisk and elegant to sweep the scree

Like the rill,like the fog of the pool,rolled and
  shrunk

Follow me to the hedge exploring your green and
  bright

I want to flare up to overturn the time and space

To be familiar with every coincidence of yours

Your smile like a half -done picture

A few strokes make your pureness,fetterless and free

Pine tree's songs and wind' s travel and chants:

Who will twinkle limpidly among the noises?
  whenever

The dusk is near the window

今夜你佇立木橋

你的夢想，你的執著與徬徨

徬徨使人擔憂

惟有星星拖曳著背影，而小雨也

悄悄地貼近我的額頭

2009.08.30作

原載臺灣《創世紀》詩雜誌，第161期，2009.12月冬季號；

轉載山東省作協主辦《新世紀文學選刊》2010.03

Tonight you stand on the wooden bridge

Your dream,your persistence and hesitance

Hesitance makes me worry

Only the stars daggle the shadow of your back,

  drizzling

Quietly soaked my forehead

刊美國 *Poems of the World*，2011春季號

十月秋雨

我記得你凝視的眼神。
你一頭微捲的褐髮，思維沉靜。
微弱的風拖在樹梢張望，
落葉在我腳底輕微地喧嚷。

你牽著我的手在畫圓，卻選擇兩平線：
銀河的一邊、數彎的濃霧、飛疾的電光，
那是我無法掌握前進的歸向，
我驚散的靈魂潛入了無明。

在山頂望夜空。從鐵塔遠眺到田野。
你的距離是無間、是無盡、是回到原點！

Autumn Rain In October

I remember your gazing eyesight

Your brown curling,your quiet thinking

The gentle wind lingering on the tip of the tree

The falling leaves whistling by the side of my feet

You take me by hand and draw the circle

Beyond the milk way, the bending thick fog, the
  sweeping lightning

There I cannot hold the direction onward

My scattered soul diving into the endless dark

Staring into the night sky on the top of the hill

From the iron tower to the far away field

The distance to you,space less,endless, back to the
  origin!

曉色的樺樹在你眼底深處雄立。

秋天的雨點在你身後串成連珠。。。。

2008.01.02作

刊登河北省作家協會《詩選刊 下半月刊》2008.第9期

The birch deeply rooted in your eye ground at draw

The drops of the autumn rain clustered by the back

   of you

雨夜

夜路中，沒有

一點人聲也沒有燈影相隨。

在山樹底盡頭，眼所觸

都是清冷，撐起

一把藍綠的小傘，等妳。

雨露出它長腳般的足跡，

細點兒地踩遍了

壘石結成的小徑，

讓我在沙泥中

心似流水般地孤寂。

我用寒衫披上了我的焦慮，

幾片落葉的微音，卻聽到

Rainy Night

On the road into the night,no

Sound ,no light shadow

Far away to the end of the trees on the hill,

Seeing all the coldness, holding

A small blue umbrella, wait for you

The rain tiptoed its long footsteps

Tiny steps and steps,trampling all around

The stony path,made me in the rough

Solitude of my heart flowing

I use my humble shirt to cover my care

The shivering leaves fall, desire to hear

那連接無盡的秋風細雨

竟在四野黯黑中出現和我一樣的心急……

2007.12作

英譯刊登美國 *Poems of the World*《世界的詩》；2010
夏季號秋季號／收錄30屆世詩會《2010世界詩選》；收錄中
國詩歌藝術學會編，《詩藝浩瀚》書籍，臺北：文史哲出版
社，2009；轉載2009.06香港《台港文學選刊》月刊2008
第9期；原載2008.02臺灣《笠》詩刊第263期，2008.02；
轉載山東省《新世紀文學選刊》2009.02；轉載中國《黃
河詩報》2009.06第5期；轉載山東《超然詩書畫》創刊號
2009.10.1

The endless autumn wind and drizzling rain

Beyond the gloomy wild with the same worry of me———

夏荷

帶著一種堅強的溫柔

從西湖中凝望

這個風月無邊的

琉璃世界

是翠鳥兒？還是岸柳拂袖

遊魚也永不疲乏的

簇擁向我

那亭台之月，悄悄披上煙霧

來看流水

就是看不盡

Summer Lotus

With gentle firmness

Sneering from the Lake West

At the endless view of

The muddy pool of

The glazed world

Is it a kingfisher

Or the floating willow on the bank

Or the tireless fish

Clustering onward

The moon above the pavilion

Quietly hiding in the cloud

Come to see the gliding water

一絲凜然的

荷影

夜的帷幕裡的光點

2008.11.27作

原載台灣《笠》詩刊，第271期，2009.06.15；刊登美國
Poems of the World《世界的詩》2010夏季號／收錄30
屆世詩會《2010世界詩選》

And the most charming and brave

The graceful shadow of lotus

Like bright stars twinkling in the dark

金池塘

風在追問杳然的彩雲
遠近的飛燕在山林的
背影掠過

羞澀的石榴
醉人的囈語，出沒的白鵝
伴著垂柳戲波

秋塘月落
鏡面，掛住的
恰是妳帶雨的明眸

2008.02.01作
原載臺灣《笠》詩刊，第265期，2008.06；轉載香港《台
港文學選刊》2008年，第9期；轉載山東省《超然詩書畫》
創刊號2009.10.01

Golden Pond

The wind is chasing the colorful clouds beyond

Far and near the shadows of the swallows

Passing by

The shy guava

The rorty raving,the hiding white goose

The weeping willows waves

The autumn pond and the falling moon

The mirror hanged

Your bright eyes with rain

流星雨

你是一把散滿霜風的
北望的弓，
那颼颼的箭
射下
簾外泣零的雪

2009.05.22作
台灣《創世紀》詩雜誌，第162期，2010.03春季刊；美國
Poems of the World《世界的詩》2010冬季號

Meteor Shower

Covered with frost and brought the wind

You, a north– directed bow

The whistling arrow

Shooting down

The sobbing snow outside the door

春已歸去

不知不覺間
托著嫩綠帶毛的小桃子
又一次，向我訴說著
一種心事

蕭蕭沙沙
麥子枯黃了
榆樹的殘花停留在四月
風總是微微的
甜甜的吹
時時送來的布穀鳥的叫聲
也沒有變

Spring Season Has Already Past

Unconsciously

Holding fluffy light green peach

Once again,you tell me

A kind of worry

Rustling and whistling

Wheat grows yellow

Withered flowers of elm lingering in April

Wind is always gentle

Blowing sweetly

Occasionally cuckoo's cooing

That will not change

春已遠去

籬笆外包圍著

一塊古老的桑田

荷葉一片二片……

浮泛在水面

而陽光正好暖和

向墻上雨痕悄然走過

2009.04.04作

臺灣《人間福報》刊登詩畫2010.5.20；香港《圓桌》詩

刊，總第26期，2009.09

Spring has already past

Outside the fence

A reach of age-old field

One or two leaves of lotus

Floating on the water——

While the warm sun light

Quietly rids the trace of rain from the wall

牧羊女的晚禱

鐘聲終於開始響了
女孩陷入沉思
從那雷雨進入尾聲的
深紫色天光
在霧般的雲朵下
傳來了天使的回音

是否我能
像這青草一般
依偎在森林的身旁？

怎樣我才能
守護沉睡中的綿羊？

Evening Prays Of The Shepherdess

At last clouts the bell

The girl falls into contemplation

From the weakening thunder storm

The modena of the daylight

Under the foggy clouds

Coming the echo of the angel

If I can

Lean close to the forest

Just like the green grass?

How can I

Guard the slept sheep?

虹的片刻安慰

嫩芽的相迎

還有那老樹

都伸出懷抱——

只有風的土氣和笨拙

帶回的訊息

干擾了我

透過這夜

這個仲夏的

晚禱

2008.07.20作

中國全國中文核心期刊山東省優秀期刊《時代文學》2009.

02月

收錄書臺灣《詩藝浩瀚》，台客編，2009.06出版

The rainbow brings forth an instant comfort

The tender bud shoots out green

And the ancient tree

All show their entertaining

Only the countrified wind shows the clumsy

He brings back the information

Disturbs me

Through the dark mist

With my mid-summer day's

Evening praying

星河

你是否來自那不變的七星潭

夜這般空明，草海桐目光澹澹

八月，波賽頓啊，讓林投之雀

在那聽雨於空穀的棲地

在那北岸的砂原後方

為黑潮的子民輕唱

有誰記得海階或碧崖

望盡雲路的傷感

任憑你來時如風浩浩

歸去又怎堪笑對故鄉

2009.08.27作

原載臺灣中國文藝協會會刊《文學人》2009.10冬季號；
〈山東省作協主辦《新世紀文學選刊》2009.文學筆會作品
選一等獎〉；中國《羊城晚報》2009.10.15；中國天津市
作協主辦《天津文學》2010.01；中國遼寧省沈陽市一級期
刊《詩潮》總第162期，2009.12

Star River

Do you come from the eternal Seven Star Lake?

So wide and bright is the night,with naupaka flowers wave

Oh, in August, Poseidon,Let the sparrows back to the
  woods

Listening to the rain in the empty valley

  and behind the northern bank of sands

Where singing for the offspring of the black waves

Who remembers the coastal terrace and the green cliff

And the sentiment of the endless road of clouds

No matter how grand like the wind when you come

Could you still smile when you leave your home

回到從前

三月

一陣風過

閃爍的螢火

溜進

我生命之夢

它們

像樹精靈

如此親切地靠近

一個記憶　　慢慢在此佇足

變成一棵水青樹

在雨露裡衰老

註：水青樹，第三紀古老子遺珍稀植物，分佈於陝西南部、甘肅東
　　南部、四川中南部和北部等地。

2010.03.03作

刊登臺灣《文學臺灣》，第75期，2010.07秋季號

Back To The Old Days

March

A blast of wind passing

Glimmering fireflies

Slip

Into my dream of life

Like the elves of the woods

So intimately approach

A memory,slowly soaked in

Changing into a green olive tree

Growing in the rain and dew

行經河深處

行經河深處

我心思索

一簇簇柳叢滴瀝著孤寂

野兔開溜在懸崖絕壁

一隻夜鴞在谷中

對著煙霧彌漫的月影搖顫

在這裡我繫不羈之心於河船

而你仍在不可知的他鄉

何曾為我守候

訴說那樸素壯麗的靈魂有多麼激昂：

天地間更沒有一顆明星

把你最深的痛苦告訴我

是怎樣的夢輕盈地落在我燃燒的心上

By The Depth Of The River

When passed the depth of the river

I stopped and thought

Tufts of willow with lonely drops

The hare gliding on the cliff

A night owl shivering in the valley

Towards the misty shadow of the moon

Here I tied my unruly heart to one boat

While you still lingering in an alien land

Never once waited for me

And talk about the passion of the splendid soul

Nor even one bright star in the sky

Pass me your deep sorrow

What an airily dream falls upon my burning heart

讓我們的愛情長成金黃的麥海

那失去驕傲，失去所有的

我，用困倦的目光，還朝著麥海繼續飛翔

2010.07.01作

刊臺灣《笠》詩刊，第280期，2010.12.15

In which our love grows into a golden sea of wheat

There pride and everything all lost

But I, with weary eyes,

  still keep on flying to the sea of the crops

懷鄉

在我飄泊不定的生涯裡
曾掀起一個熟悉的聲音
但不久便重歸寂靜

它從何而來？
竟使我深深的足跡追影不及……
游啄的目光分離成渺遠的印記
每一步都是那麼堅定無疑

呵，我心戚戚
那是深夜傳來淒清的弦子
我識得，但如何把窺伺的黎明矇蔽

2010.01.11作
原載臺灣《新原人》2010年夏季號，第70期；轉載中國山東
省作協主辦《新世紀文學選刊》2010.03期

Homesickness

In my wandering life

Once raised a familiar voice

But soon returned to quietude

Where did it come from?

It urged my steps hurrying forward

It separated my eyesight into vague impression

Every step is solid and firm

Oh, my sorrowful heart

Listen to the miserable chord of the night

But how can I blind the peering dawn

聲音在瓦礫裡化成泣雪

聲音在瓦礫裡化成泣雪，
在強震後的秋夜
此刻倘有些許月光，
樹影便已慌亂。

鏽般的天空一片死寂，
那看不見的哀懇
不時偃伏
讓黎明舉步維艱。

2010.10.02作
刊登臺灣《笠》詩刊，279期，2010.10.15

Vox In Debris Melted Into Weeping Snow

Vox in debris melted into weeping snow

In autumn night after the strong shock

A slice of moonlight this moment

And flustering shadow of the tree

Rusty night is deathly still

Grief and mourning is unseen

Lay down here every now and then

Stumbling the steps of the dawn

海上的中秋

新雨乍晴，
遠山不染纖塵，
竟映照一抹閃紅，
點亮在古剎楊樹上。

風柔柔，四野寂然
只有白浪無止無息
憑依暮鼓聲聲。

我在霧中走著，
想摭拾一串串星顆，
讓階前草露的微音
隨風而去；
在霜徑菊香裡，
也在明月外。

《天津文學》2010.01

Mid-Autumn Day On The Sea

The newly fined day after the rain

The distant mountain is washed clean and pure

It mirrors a smear of flash red

Lightening the poplars of the old temple

The wind is gentle,the wildness is silent

Only the white waves rolling

Mixed with the sound of the evening drums

Walking in the fog

I want to pick up a string of stars

And listen to the passing whisper of the grass

I'm inside the path of dew with fragrance of

  chrysanthemum

And also outside the bright and distant moon

遙寄商禽

你是碧潭湖上的秋月，
宙斯殿上的黎明，
白色山脈裡孤挺的蒼松，
凝視著遠方的一朵落櫻。

星光下金灣裡吟遊篇篇，
紫光的雲，虹橋的天，
從容的風輕吻你的髮，
在你乾澀的臉頰上。

天使的牽迎，上帝的垂憐，
你的眼睛背後

To Shangqin Far Away

You are the autumn moon upon the green Lake,
The dawn of the Temple of Zeus,
The lonely green pine tree in the white mountain,
A falling petal of cherry staring into the far.

Under the starlight you wonder
  and chant in the Golden Bay.
The clouds are purple, the sky is rainbow,
With gentle breeze kissing your hair,
And your dry cheeks.

God blesses you ,the angel leads you,
Behind your eyes your sorrow,

恰有哀愁似灰藍深海，

刺穿了我空懸的早晨的詩泉。

2010.09.05作

臺灣《文學臺灣》第77期，2011.01春季號；轉載中國文藝
協會會刊《文學人》季刊，革新版第9期

Is like the deep blue-gray ocean ,

Piercing through my vacant poetic spring in the morn.

我不嘆息、注視和嚮往

古老的村塘

凝碧在田田的綠荷上

我們曾經雀躍地踏遍它倒影的淺草

看幾隻白鴨

從水面銜起餘光

一個永遠年輕卻不再激越的回音

在所有的漣漪過後　猶響

2010.05.15作

刊登中國天津市作協主辦《天津文學》2011.01期

No Sigh,Gaze And Proceed

The ancient pond in the village

A coagulation upon the leaves of the lotus

We once cheerfully trod on the weeds

  of the inverted reflection in the pond

And saw white ducks passing

Picking up the setting sunlight from the water

An echo forever young yet no more agitation

Still resounding after all the ripples passed

拂曉之前

沒一點雜色

林中

點點水光忽隱忽顯

鬱鬱杜松

孕出螞蟻的卵

隨荊棘聲愜意地伸長

一叢野當歸縮在樹牆旁幽坐

像是沉醉於

命運的遐想

2010.02.30作

原載臺灣《文學台灣》季刊，2010.04夏季號，第74期；轉載新疆省《綠風》詩刊，2010.05.10第3期，總第189期

Dawning

Not a bit of mottle

The forest

With twilight and shimmering

An elegant hackmatack

Gestate offspring of the ants

Stretching out with thorns in a cozy way

A cluster of wild angelica sitting by the tree

Seems still indulge in dreaming

About its fate and fortune

原鄉
──詠六堆

吹綠了圍屋的風，你不再要四處流浪，
你已經停歇於忠義祠的肩胛，群星醒轉；
秋祭，空氣的寂靜等著你腳步到來，
我的雙眼便浮現了晶瑩的騰躍……

吹綠了柵門的風，堅韌且悠揚，
你已經熟悉於每一橫巷舊事的片斷；
夜晚，飽滿而平柔的月亮親吻城牆的時候
我的額頭便貼滿甜眠的榮光……

你是如此純淨，如此寬廣，又不經意地
出現，向著我的靈魂張望，
那可是你經過的金色的季節，
敲響出我最深邃的餘音和田園的吟唱？

Chant Of Liu Dui

Oh,wind,you has changed the surrounding green,

  do not wander again,

You has rested on the shoulders of the temple of loyalty,

  see the stars waking;

In the memorial ceremony of autumn,

  the quietness is waiting for your steps,

Then before my eyes there are glittering and translucent

  prances;

Oh,wind,you has changed the fences green, you

  diligent and melodious,

You has got to know all the dribs and drabs of the old

  legends ;

2009.11.15作

原載臺灣《笠》詩刊，第277期，2010.06.15；臺灣中國文
藝協會會刊《文學人》2009.11革新版，第7期；轉載武漢市
第一大報《長江日報》2009.11.20；山東省作協主辦《新
世紀文學選刊》2010.03

When the full moon gently kisses the city wall in the
  evening,
My forehead is covered with glory of sweet sleep......

You are so pure,so broad,and unexpectedly,
  appeared,glimpsing at my soul,
Is that the golden season you passed through,
Knocking out my deepest aftersound and the pastoral
  singing?

一切都在理性的掌握中

我的夢海，沒有奇突的劇情

有的只是用心去尋找

那掌握不住的永恆

當你眼底的憂鬱

將兩個世紀的神話連接在一起

以綠色的翅翼

恰似稻穗上的蝗蟲正閃動而出

從時空的迷失中醒來

這個世界僅僅在

倒影上傾斜了一瞬間

那輕舟

披著真愛的風

劃開了真實與虛幻

一切都在理性的掌握中

Everything In Rational Control

My dream of sea,No splashing guts

Only the eternity beyond control

That can be found with sincere heart

When the gloom in your eyes

Connect the myths of two centuries

With green wings

Just like locusts flickering on ears of crops

Awaking from the lost of time and space

The world only be there

A flash of the slant of the shadow

The canoe

Wraps around within sincere love

Dividing the truth from the fancy

Everything in rational control

再一次，生命之帆

像蝌蚪一樣經過蛻變

宛如雪山之巔的歌雀──

愛琴海的時代倒流

是風車在低訴歷史

用諸島的目光

是山頂的鐘塔在敲響

歲月無痕的沉重

而那蔚藍還在天空

墨綠也還座落在山坡上

但我美麗的，心痛的記憶啊

Once again,the sail of life

Like the tadpole's spallation

As it were the singing bird on snow mountain crest

Flowing backwards of the Aegean times

The telling of the past by the windmills

In the sight of the islands

The knocking from the bell tower on the mountaintop

The heaviness of the traceless years

Yet the luxuriant blue is still in the sky

The jasper is still spreading on the hillside

But my beautiful,painful memory

是那樣脆弱而貧乏

早就被那抹金陽的微笑

沖淡在枝葉掩映中

2010.06.29作

臺灣《創世紀》詩雜誌2010年冬季號，165期

So fragile and indigent

Already diluted by the smile of the golden sun

Covered in the shadow of leaves

山楂樹

我在暮色中網住一隻鳥
它有秋月般的暈黃
虹彩般的髮
我願意朝夕地守望
每當它迅速地
驕矜地
把一個白霜的山丘
圈在它的腳踝上

春神在我臂下休息
仲夜從我身邊溜去
我沿著小路沒有回頭
直想輕步接近它的孤獨身軀
冬風不停地呼嘯而去

Hawthorn Tree

In the twilight I netted a bird

Its fluffy yellow likes the autumn moon

Its feather the color of rainbow,

I'd rather keep watching day and night

Each time when it suddenly

Proudly

Tie the hoarfrost covered hill

To its tarsus

The goddess of Spring rests under my arms

Midnight gliding away by my side

I walk along the path without looking back

Only think of approaching its lonely stature

Winter whistling and howling and passing

但我只能前行
直到它帶回長長的回音：
呵，忘卻你，忘卻我……
──是動中無聲的安寧

2010.12.19作
臺灣《創世紀》詩雜誌2011.03春季號，第166期

Until it brings back the long echoing

Ah,forgive you,and forgive me——

Only the peace in the moving silence——

綠淵潭

若沒了這群山脈，恐怕你將分不清
通向另一片蔚藍的希望之船，
那裡黎明正在沾滿白雪的雲階上等你。

總是，在分別的時刻才猛然想起
潭邊小屋恬靜地下著棋，當晚星
把你從落了葉的岳樺樹後帶往我身邊，
別憂懼，我已沿著那隱蔽的淒清昏光
滑入閃爍的冰叢外虛寂的海洋。

2010.06.24作
臺灣《創世紀》詩雜誌2010冬季號，165期

Green Deep Pond

Without the ranges of the mountains,

perhaps you could not distinguish,

The ship of hope sailing to another blue sea,

Where the dawn is waiting for you on the stairs of clouds

  covered with white snow.

For ever,only when parting it may suddenly occur

Quietly playing chess in the cottage by the pond,

  when evening star

Bringing you to me from behind the leafless Yuehua

  birch to me,

No worry,Along the faint light from the shady I have

  slided

Into the vacant sea outside the sparkling cluster of ice.

海祭

福爾摩莎

不經意地醒來

那虹橋的餘光

是青巒間

一隻掙扎的小螢蛾

當冬陽升起時

我的眼淚

你的觸撫

多喜樂

如母親眼底的溫柔

The Fete Of The Sea

Formosa

Wakes up casually

The split vision of the rainbow bridge

Is a struggled firebug

Among the green mountain

When the winter sun rises

My tears

And your feeling

How much rejoice and pleasure

Like the warm in mother's eyes

在這無晴的蒼穹

多少世情的虛空

巡行著……

2010.12.16作

刊登臺灣《創世紀》詩雜誌2011.03春季號，第166期

In the semi-dark welkin

How much hollowness of the world

Patrolling——

等候黎明

把對岸的屋宇加點光
鐵窗割切成
紙畫

乃至欸乃一聲
方驚醒
今夜月光如利刃
已劃過數不盡的
年

風吹散每一嘆息
都那樣久遠久遠了

Waiting For The Dawning

Adding some light to the thither house

The iron window cuts it into

paper painting

Untill the sound of singing with oaring

Wake up with a start

Tonight the moon light a sword

Already cut through countless

Years

Wind blowing away every sigh

All are long distant away

是明天，且期待重生

親愛的，你會來嗎？

2007.11.22作

香港大公報編印《黃河詩報》，總第5期，2009.06

Tomorrow, waiting for the rebirth

My beloved, are you coming ?

淵泉

涼晨中
我聽見流泉就在前方
仿若一切拂逆與困厄
全都無懼地漂走

一隻信鴿在白樺樹林頻頻
投遞
春的祭典

我相信悲傷的愛情
它隨著蒼海浮光
有時擱淺在礁岸
隨沙礫嘎啦作響

2010.01.04作
香港《香港文學》2010.03

Deep Spring

Cold morning

I hear the flowing spring ahead

As if the frustrations and distresses

All float away fearlessly

A white dove among the silver birches frequently

Delivering

The fiesta of spring

I believe in the melancholy of love

It drifts along with the shimmering of the sea

Sometimes piles up on the shore

Uttering a clacking sound along with the gravel

縱然剎那

湖面滿是薄染

將落的金光

讓淺玫瑰的雲霞

溶在銀波上

遠山幾行

有如紫精屏風的灰綠

遠比星空更柔然無聲的顫動

動蕩的一桅風帆

半湖碧水

不若你明眸的閃爍

在影落波間

我感到宇宙只此一刻

春風拂來

Even If Only In A Flash

The lake is fully covered with thin tinge

The setting golden light

Melting the pink roses of clouds

In the silver waves

Lines of distant mountains

Like the grayish-green of the amethyst screen

The shivering far more gentle and noiseless than the

  starry sky

The turbulent mast of the sail

The blue water of half of the lake

Can not compare your twinkling eyes

Among the falling shadows and between the waves

I feel the flash of the universe

我已幻成白楊之林

昂首矗立

在湖畔旁等候月光

原載安徽省文聯主辦《安徽文學》2010.1-2期；轉載北京市
中國人民大學書報資料中心主辦《當代文萃》；2010.04，
總第138期，頁62

With the spring breeze whisking

I melted into the illusion of a forest of poplar

Proudly stand tall and upright

Waiting for the show of the moonlight to the lake

月森林

晚鐘續續之
敲聲。偶一回頭
即不復寐

仰望那
瑩白的天空
卻有一枚圓月
濛濛在不凋的今夜

2009.03.26作
香港《香港文學》2010.03

Moon Forest

The curfew echoing

Knocking sound . Turn back by chance

No longer sleep

Looking up

The silvering sky

With one full moon

Mistily shines in the endless night

靜寂的黃昏

一隻秋鷺立著，它望著遠方。

萋萋的蘆葦上一葉扁舟。

對岸：羊咩聲，鼓噪四周的蛙鳴。

它輕輕地振翅飛走，

羽毛散落苗田，

彷彿幾絲村舍的炊煙。

2010.2.20作

原載臺灣《創世紀》詩雜誌，2010.06夏季號；轉載臺灣
《人間福報》副刊2011.05.30

The Still Dusk

An egret stands,watching far away

Among the luxuriant reeds a leaf of flat boat

On the other shore : baaing of the sheep,

  clamour of the croaks of the frogs around

Flapping the wings gently it flies away

Only a few feathers falling down to the fields

As if the threads of smoke from kitchen chimneys of

  the cottage

凝

這一畦稻浪

隨牛背上的炊煙飄來⋯⋯

泊在水月裡

我想起幼時木麻黃下的鞦韆

螢火蟲躲閃著

到哪兒去？在風中踏響

那步履兒

可是踽踽而行的母親

而不安的亮星

於山村的木橋上

多了些牽掛

2009.12.28作

原載《香港文學》2010.03；轉載山東省作協主辦《新世紀

文學選刊》2010.03

Gazing

Waves of the rice field shimmering

Along with the drift of the cooking smoke of

  buffalo's back——

Berthing by the moon of the water

I remember the swing under the casuarina in my early

  days

Firefly twinkling

Where to go? Steps sounding in the wind

Are the steps

Mummy's slow walking

The uneasy stars bright

Upon the wooden bridge of the mountain village

Some more worries and cares

刹那

當2:56劇晃的瞬間

大海忽地

伸出千萬隻猙獰的爪

撲地而來

星空下地貌已模糊不清

哪裡是我美麗的夢園？

何處尋我歸來的愛戀？

那清晰如昨的呼吶

在四野中瘋長

天遙處尚有嗚咽的雲

低婉地訴說——啊眼已灼熱

此一別，丘上

的櫻花

盡情為我而落

A Blink

Fifty-six minute past two,a blink's severe shake

The sea suddenly

Stretch out millions of ferocious claws

Rushing on the ground

Blurring the fields under the starlit sky

Where is my beautiful dreamland?

How can I find my returned love?

Yesterday's crying is still so clear

Crazily growing in the wild field

Sobbing clouds lingering by the far distance

Murmuring——hot tears are bursting

Farewell, cherry blossoms on the hillock

For me, you fall as much as you can

Broken walls of the balefire concealed away

烽火的斷牆隱隱遠去

已輻射不到春天泥塑般僵硬的表情

是誰誦經聲

——隨風的背影走近

啊生命蒼涼

願為故土中

一粒柔軟的征塵

2011.03.25追悼日本311震變而作

臺灣《人間福報》2011.04.25

It can not radiate the stiff expressions

  of the clay sculpture in spring

Who is reciting Buddhist sutras

Approaching with the shadow of the wind

Oh,bleak life

I want to change to soft dust settled in journey

Buried in the earth of my homeland

中秋懷想

我不知道

故鄉的夜蟬 是否

還是蕩氣迴腸

一壺老白茶

沏著舊時光

我不知道

記憶的小河 是否

還是靜靜流淌

今夜舊街巷

光芒或淡黯

我不知道

夢裡的人兒 是否

Nostalgia At Mid- Autumn Day

I don't know

Whether the night cicadas in the hometown

Still singing the soul-stirring melody

A pot of old white tea

Making the tea of the old time

I don't know

Whether the stream of my memory

Still flowing quietly

The old street tonight

Shining brightly or hiding in the dark

I don't know

Whether the man in my dream

還是舉杯邀月

對影共桂香

如果每頁歷史

都無法觸摸到

世事與滄桑

那麼明日何妨

更待銀河　溯流而上

2011.8.24

刊登臺灣《人間福報》副刊2011.9.12中秋節

Still toasting the moon

  with his shadow they drink

In the fragrance of the laurel

If every page of history

Cannot touch

The glimpse of the moon and change

Then why not tomorrow

Roaming the galaxy upstream

雨後的夜晚

雪松寂寂

風裏我

聲音在輕喚著沉睡的星群

梧桐也悄然若思

路盡處，燈火迷茫

霧中

一個孤獨的身影

靜聽蟲鳴

雕像上的歌雀

狡黠又溫熙地環伺著

Night After The Rain

The pine tree with snow was still

The wind is embracing me

A voice is gently calling the slept stars

Phoenix trees are also thinking

The light is dim at the end of the road

In the fog

A lonely figure

Listening to the chirps of the insects

The nightingale on the statue

Circling around craftily and brightly

突然，一陣樂音

隨夜幕飛來……拉長了小徑

2010.11.6

刊登臺灣《海星》詩刊，2011.08創刊號

Suddenly ,a hail of music

Flying over with the night,——stretching the trail

along

在初冬湖濱

聽，雪中雲雀的足音

梅朵輕嘆兀自凋零

宛如夜行而過

急速消失的螢蟲

四野望去，盡是

空寂的淡色，只有

遠山帶著半黃

半紅的背影，引我步出了樹林

西天被幾聲犬號擊破

朝陽在半壁，不甘

蟄伏，掙扎著探出頭

我，將粘上衣襟的湖光

還於金色的謐靜

On The Lake Bank In Early Winter

Listen,the voice of the lark in the snow

Plum blossoms sigh,withered lonely away

As if passing at night

Swiftly vanished Firefly

Looking around,only the

Empty tinge,none but

The far off mountain with semi-yellow

Semi-red shadow ,lead me step out of the woods

The western sky is torn by a few dogs' barking

The rising sun shines on the half-cliff,not willing

To hibernate ,struggling to stretch out its head

Me,return the ray of the lake on my shirt

To the golden quietness

走進夢想，且

讓過去的種種，化成

心頭的澄澈

當黎明升起——

我在水銀裡呼

吸，一股稻草甘甜的

清香，自空氣中凝聚……

2009.01.22作

刊登全國中文核心期刊，山東省優秀期刊《時代文學》

2009.2期；臺灣《人間福報》2009.9.4

Walk into the dream,and

Let the variety of the past melting

Into the clarity of the mind

When it dawns——

I shall call from the quicksilver

Take in,the sweet fragrance of the straw

The faint scent,condensing from the air......

回憶的沙漏

回憶的沙漏

滴滴滴下，似淚成河

我整夜輾轉反側

那小路上閃現的星光

是夏夜在那裡眯著眼

從天幕的破處

傳來聲聲呼喚，縱橫錯落

大地上一切已從夢中醒覺

山影終將無法藏匿

我卻信，我將孤獨痛苦地

漫行於沙漠世界

The Sandglass Of The Memory

The sandglass of the memory

Drop by drop,like the tears of the river

All night long I'm tossing about

The shining starlit of the path

Is that the twinkling eyes of the summer night

Down from the split of the screen of the sky

Waves of calling ,strew at random

All on the earth are already waking

The shadow of the mountain could no longer hide

I believe,I 'll wander to the world of desert

With loneliness and painfulness

夜，依然濃重

徜徉於

白堤的浮萍之間

2010.07.09作

登臺灣《創世紀》詩雜誌2010.09秋季號，164期

The night,still dense

Roaming

In between the duckweeds of the white banks

雲豹

靜靜地伏趴

橫向的粗枝上

縱目四方

來自老山

如黑環帶的勇士

有著洞悉靈魂的冷靜

在叫做小鬼湖林道

流於族人的傳說──

我的爪牙自皮鞘中伸出

獵物在濃密的倒木裡竄躲

啊，奔馳的笑聲已成塵土

只有魯凱祖靈與我細數足印

而那遠離的人類不再

Clouded Leopard

Quietly pronate upon

A transverse thick branch

Looking as far as my eyes can see

Coming from the old mountains

Like the warrior with the black belt

Holding the calmness and discerning the soul

In the woods by the Pixy lake

Flowing in the legend of the clansmen

My paws and fangs out from the sheath

My preys flee and hide among bushy fallen trees

Oh,the galloping laughter has turned to dust

With me the Spirits of Rukai count the footprints

While the removed mankind no longer

以槍及牟利的藉口
然後在星空那端悠悠蕩蕩地出現
一道無所畏懼的眼色

2009.02.13作
刊登臺灣《笠》詩刊第272期，2009.08.15；美國《臺灣公
論報》2010.8.13刊登莫渝評論此詩

With the excuses of gun and profits

Then in the starlit sky floating about

And casting down a fearless glance

每當黃昏飄進窗口⋯⋯

常青藤種子開始酣睡

松針的氣味總是

穿牆破隙

刺亂我的衫袖⋯⋯

尤其在夜裡與融雪之後

儘管它們就在屋外的彎路

離我只有咫尺之隔

我還是喜歡偷偷地眺望

恣意的松鼠到處採擷

遺落的球果

當我腳底裹上驚奇並浸染

枝頭的木香

Whenever The Dusk Floating Into The Window

Seeds of ivies begin to sleep

Always the scent of pine needles

Pull through the wall

Prick into the sleeves

Especially when night and the melting snow

Although they are on the crooked road outside the room

At a distance of a few feet and inches

I still like to view it on the sneak

The reckless squirrels gather the nuts

And the falling cones everywhere

When the surprise wrapped my feet and soaked
  through

四野的生物彷彿重新敞開

一種香甜而富饒的感覺

如同被石壁的回音所彈奏

它像崖邊的流雲般孤獨

也像古老的豎琴那樣沉碧

每當黃昏飄進我的窗口……

我將松針藏在那

苦澀的地土之中

2009.11.01作

山東省作協主辦《新世紀文學選刊》2010.03期

The sweet-smell spreading over the branches

All the creatures around seem to come to again

A rich feeling fragrant and sweet

Seems to be echoed from the rocks of the hills

It is as lonesome as the drifting clouds by the cliff

And also like the ancient harp profound and bluish

Whenever the dusk floating into my window

I will conceal the pine needles there

Beneath the saline soil of the land

岸畔

一隻松鼠
倒懸
不露生色的天空。

它竄來跳去，無視
跌宕紅塵
唯有鳥影打破沉默。

我在岸畔行走
撈捕：風的腳履兒
深一步，淺一步
時光的蜻羽輕輕凝固。

On The Bank

A squirrel

Hangs upside down

Under the cover of the dim sky

Jumps here and there,ignoring

Ups and downs of the mortals

Only the birds' shadow piercing

I walk on the bank

Fishing for :steps of the wind

One step deep,one step shallow

Quietly clotted the dragonfly's wing

偶抬眼，綠芭蕉升上

春之草垛

在裸石後染亮了。

2010.03.13作

原載臺灣《笠》詩刊，281期，2011.02.15；轉載美國《新
大陸》詩刊，122期，2011.02.30

By chance to view,green bananas tall

Haystacks of spring

Tinged bright behind the stones

在雕刻室裡

天窗下的那雙手

全神貫注地

　　有如碼頭上的一盞燈

從孤寂海洋

　　凝視記憶裡的小徑

沒人看到這個老人

燭光底下幾近透明的

臉及深碧的眼睛

啊，今晚且讓我的愛

也歪斜在空中敲響，叮叮噹噹……

2010.12.26作

──臺灣《文學臺灣》2011夏季號，第78期

In The Room Of Carving

The hands under the skylight

In rapt Concentration

As if the light on the dock

From the lonely ocean

Gazing for the path in the mind

No one has seen the old man

Under the candlelight almost lucid

  face and pure green eyes

Ah,tonight let my love

Also slant and ring in the sky,clinking......

在交織與遺落之間

秋夜在交織與遺落之間徘徊，
與它暈染的霜葉相戀。
那是我曾在夢境中尋覓過的
世界在那裡是寂靜的
只要我想許願，它就近在咫尺
又何必捨近慕遠？

在那裡，一切都可顯現──
風語，胡楊，長河，月亮灣……
都歇息於喚你名字的輪迴。
然後在遠離牧道的地方，我醒來
時間卻已重複
像駝鈴般同樣孤零的音旋。

Between Interlace And Miss

Autumn night lingers between interlace and miss

It falls in love with its frost-tinged maple leaves

That is what I have sought in my dreams

There is the peaceful and quiescent world

So long as I want to promise ,so long as it will be near by

Why should I abandon the nearby to seek something

  far away?

Over there,everything is visualized——

Whistling wind,poplars,long river,the bay of the

  moon......

All rest upon the whirligig calling for your name

Then far away from the path of the pastureland,

  I wake up

是光把冰冷的書頁轉變成

青鳥悠然遨翔於雲天，

讓我的思想越過了彩虹——

尋覓一處如你盯視的眼眸的重叠。

如果愛情也能時刻散佈

那麼，為何我仍停頓又走動於人間？

2010.08.02作

臺灣《笠》詩刊，第281期，2011.02.15

Yet time has overlapped

Like the notes of the lonely bells of the camels

  circling

It is the light who turns the ice-cold pages into

Blue birds flying freely in the sky

Let my ideas soar upon the rainbow——

Look for one place like the overlap of the gazing of

  your eyes

If love can also be scattered around at any time

Then,why should I pause and move in the world?

兩岸青山連天碧
——陪海基會走過二十年感時

多少次坐在歷史之岸尋舊夢

走過的風雨如昨日，月

凝神，遠山長滿相思

我把天際撥開，便覺香江不再遙遠

島嶼在頻頻傳遞，重續探親的

驚喜，落雪轉眼飄成白桐

多少人正開始寄盼

春從一笑後姍姍而來

我將希望之燈點燃，無視

時光悠遠，別後生命蒼涼之悲

每當四野的音樂吹響

Formosa就以遼闊之藍，和雲朵競著唱和

Green Mountains Along The Banks Under The Blue Sky

——For the companionship of SEF
for 20 years

How many times sitting on the bank of history

 dreaming

The wind and storms seem to be yesterday,the moon

With fixed attention,the far away mountains grow

 with longing

I roll up the sky,and find the Xiang River is no longer

 far away

The island is frequently passing on, people go home again

The surprise ,snowflakes in a blink dye phoenix trees white

How many people are expecting the start

Spring slowly comes with the smile

I light the lamp of hope, not to think

The long time,the sadness of the bleak life when depart

多少回我似無家的風在林間低回

世間又有哪一朵雲，能歸後

再相逢？那淡漠的天空是否也

咀嚼著低吟的自由？

每當白鴿把

和平之鐘叩響時，山和水便合十了

啊，太平洋柔柔的海波

是否牽掛我第一次俯瞰母親

做大海之遊？

聽，那地母懷裡是否也有喜樂的心音？

那祖靈庇護的——

是否讓所有的言語都能融合你我

Whenever the music echoes all around

Formosa will compete with the clouds in the chorus

  based on its blue of the sea

How many times I drift like homeless wind in the

  woods

Which cloud in the sky can return and meet again?

If the cool welkin is also

  Chewing the croon of freedom?

Every time pigeons knock

  the bell of peace,the mountain and the river

Will put the palms together

Ah,the gentle waves of the Pacific Ocean

If you care my first overlook of my mother

因為愛

能戰勝隔絕近半世紀的恐懼

如母親眼底的溫柔，今天我就要踏回故鄉

噢，親愛的，你是否

如滿天星斗早已守候：又或許

春神也執起牧鞭，整裝待發了

2010.12.06作

臺灣《人間福報》2011.3.7

and take the voyage?

Listen,if a cheerful and hearty voice also cherished by the

   mother of the land?

If what is protected by the ancestors——

Will link you and me with all the words and expressions

For love

Can conquer the fear which makes isolation for half

   a century

With the kindness from the mother,today I will go home

Oh, my dear, if you

Like the starlit sky waiting for a long time, or perhaps

God of Spring also hold the herding whip, ready and

   waiting

懷舊

往事是光陰的綠苔，
散雲是浮世的飄蓬。
雞鳴，我漫不經心地步移，
春歸使我愁更深。

一花芽開在我沉思之上，
孕蕾的幼蟲在悄然吐絲；
它細訴留痕的愛情，
縷縷如長夜永無開落。

2009.09.24作
刊登《香港文學》2010.03期；臺灣《秋水》146期2010.07；
轉載山東省作協主辦《新世紀文學選刊》2010.03；湖南省
《愛你》係湖南教育報刊社與湖北日報傳媒集團；《特別關
注》雜誌社聯合辦刊。2010.第7期

Nostalgia

Bygones are the green moss of the time

Floating clouds are the fleabanes of the vanity of the
  world

Rooster crowing,I move my steps unconcernedly

Spring returning makes me even more worried

A flower bud blossoms in my contemplation

A grub on the sprout quietly spins

It details its love story which carves trace in life

Continuously like the long night never end

秋日的港灣

流動的時光羅織著晚浪

與幽微的漁火。

一片無人注意的蚵棚，

在鹹澀的雨中。

蘆花迴蕩的挽歌

被秋風輕輕挾起，移步向前。

古堡則把我的眼波下錨

繫住所有的懷念。

2010.02.21作

臺灣《乾坤》詩刊2011春季號，第57期

Harbor In Autumn Days

Harbor In autumn days

Floating time nets the evening tides

And the dim lights on fishing boats

A reach of un-noticed shed of oyster

Soaked in the salty and astringent rain

Reverberating the elegies of the reeds

Raised up by the autumn wind gently ,and pushed

  forward

The old castle anchorages the waves of my eyes

Holding all of my yearns and memories

午夜

隨之躍起的繁星中我銜起樹濤聲

久久佇立，以雲遮棚

那曾經飛翔之夢

忽湧到心頭

在柔風中飄動

但我不能劃破這靜謐

在幽思綿綿中

生命已無籲求，我是醒著的

2010.06.22作

臺灣《新原人》2010.夏季號，第70期

Midnight

Along with the rising stars, I take up the billows

  of the woods

Standing for long, clouds as my shed

The dream once soaring

Pouring into my heart

Waving in the breeze

Yet can't tear the silence

In the unbroken pondering

My life desires nothing,and I'm awake

岸畔之樹

在我憩息的地方
岸畔之樹
像潺潺小溪
流經大片花田般
圍繞著我奏樂
在寂靜的森林內輕響

呵，那水貂似的髮絲
——我難尋踪跡的女孩
依著風的手指
忽隱忽現
快速地
問訊而來

Tree On The Bank

In the place I rest

A tree by the bank

Like a rippling river

Flowing through a reach of flower field

Surround me and play music

Gently echoes in the quiet woods

Oh,my girl ,your shining hair like a mink

——hard for me to find you

Following the finger of the wind

Flickering

Fleetly

Come for inquiry

只一瞬間

黑瞳晶若夜雪

妳是海

你是樹心

不，不是，你是輕風吹拂的白罌粟

我的一切，繆斯無法增添你一分光彩

2010.07.13作

臺灣《創世紀》詩雜誌2010.09秋季號，第164期

Only a blink

Your black pupils the shining snowy night

You are the sea

You are the heart of the tree

Oh, no, you are a white poppy fluttering in the breeze

You are all to me，the Muse can add no more to

　your brilliance

北埔夜歌

水車舞弄的夜，

透明得像淚珠潮湧；

牌樓悵然，山芙蓉低吟：

九降風，很難盲從——

在幽微的義民祭，

誰的舊事比北埔更雋永？

我的先民，我的鄉夢，誰能

洗滌你眼底的真淳

並將兩個世紀的時空深烙於此刻？

以沿溪的花謝花開，

家廟前的雨正搖曳走過，

迎向巡禮的天燈的灼熱；

The Song Of Beipu At Night

The night stirred by the water mills

As transparent as the pouring drops of tears

Decorated archways gloomy, hibiscus croons

Wind of September,not to follow blindly

At the sacred Justice Folk Fiesta

Whose past more meaningful than Beipu?

My ancestors, my dream of the home, who can

Wash your sincereness from your eyes

And carve time and space of two centuries on this
   moment ?

With the flowers blooming and withering along the river

The rain in front of the Ancestral temple joggling away

Facing the blazing heat of the patrolling lights in the sky

愛人啊，自從雙眸

不再許我隔世的輕愁，

在不乏堅毅的話語裡，

只對老街、小巷、為明天擁抱天空！

哪怕多少年後每一憶想

總在我耳邊放歌升騰……

2009.11.18作

原載台灣中國文藝協會會刊《文學人》季刊，2009年11月冬季號；轉載《澳華日報》406期2009.12；轉載山東省作協主辦《新世紀文學選刊》2010.03

Oh, my love, since your eyes

No more permition for my worry of the long past

The firm and persistent words

Only for the old street, alley, and embrace the sky for

tomorrow!

Even if after many years to recall

It will always sing and leap up by my ears——

黃昏是繆斯沉默的眼神

黃昏是繆斯沉默的眼神……

風高坐在樹巔上

描著蛋彩的畫布，像往日般

候著雲霓，這是六月的港灣

夜挨近，一聲汽笛穿林而過

這或許是

無盡的岸邊甜美的呼喚

我的愛

猶然迴響

烙在泛黃的秸稈中

2010.06.10作

山東省作協主辦《新世紀文學選刊》2010.03增刊號

The Dusk Is The Silent Expression In Muse's Eyes

The dusk is the silent expression in Muse 's eyes

The wind sits high on the top of the tree

Drawing the canvas with colors,as usual

Waiting for the rosy clouds,the bay of June

Night approaching,a whistle goes through the forest

Perhaps it is

Melting calling from the endless bank

My love

Just as the echoes

Cauterized into the yellowing straw

四月的夜風

悠悠地，略過松梢

充滿甜眠和光，把地土慢慢蘇復

光浮漾起海的蒼冥

我踱著步。水聲如雷似的

切斷夜的偷襲

我聽見

野鳩輕輕地低喚，與

唧唧的蟲兒密約

古藤下，我開始想起

去年春天。你側著頭

回眸望一回，你是凝，是碧翠

是一莖清而不寒的睡蓮！

The Night Wind Of April

Leisurely, passes the tip of the pine tree

Full of sweet sleep and light,gently waking the land

Ripples brighten the dark green of the sea

I pace along. The water sounds like thunders

Cutting the still hunt of the night

I hear

Wild cooers cooing,and

The chirping worms date

Under the old vine, I begin to think

Last spring. You turn your head aside

Look back once, you are the gazing,the green jade

A clear but not cold pond lily!

這時刻，林裡。林外

星子不再窺視於南窗

而我豁然瞭解：

曾經有絲絲的雨，水波拍岸

在採石山前的路上……

2009.04.08作

中國遼寧省沈陽市一級期刊《詩潮》，總第162期，

2009.12；新疆《綠風》詩刊2010.05第3期，總第189期；

山東省作協主辦《新世紀文學選刊》2010.03；臺灣《人間

福報》副刊2010.4.19

This moment, inside the woods. Outside it

Stars no more peer into the southern window

I'm suddenly enlightened:

There are once drizzling rain, the waves to the shore

On the road in front of the mountain to the quarry ——

瓶中信

緊抱僅有的一線

希望，寄託波浪

她傳遞的使命，

支撐著夢想。

風霜的臉 佈滿了驟雨，

強忍著痛。

一座冰山 擋在她的胸口，

請求通航。

風知道她來自古老的故鄉

歷經萬險

The Letter In The Bottle

Grasp tight the thread

Of hope,bailment in the waves

Her mission of transfer

Supporting the dream

The weather-beaten face is washed by the storm

Struggling to endure the painfulness

An iceberg blocks in her chest

Praying for the opening of the navigation

Wind knows the old hometown she comes from

Go through all the hardships

只為一個不變的諾言，
像一個月亮。

2008.01作
轉載中國全國中文核心期刊，山東省優秀期刊《時代文學》
期刊2009.02；收錄2008年《臺灣文學年鑑》，彭瑞金編，
頁119-121詩五首之一；轉載香港《台港文學選刊》，2008
年第9期；轉載中國《黃河詩刊》2009年總5期；原載臺灣
《葡萄園》詩刊，177期，2008.05夏季號

For one unchangeable faith

Like the bright moon

雲淡了，風清了

把愛琴海上諸神泥塑成圓頂的鐘塔
回歸
寧靜

你看，那夕陽下的風車
天真地在海邊唱遊
那碧波的點點白帆
輕撫著客中的寂寞

啜著咖啡；青天
自淺紅
至深翠
沖淡濃潤的綠，白色的牆

The Cloud Is Light,
The Wind Is Gentle

Clay sculptured the Gods of aegean sea into vaulted
  clock tower
Returning
To tranquility

You see, the windmill in the setting sun
Naively singing and playing by the sea
White sails floating over the blue waves
Comforting the loneliness of the guests

Sipping coffee; blue sky
From shallow red
To deep green
Diluting thick green, white wall

耳際只有草底的鳴蟲

抑抑悲歌……

2007.11.21作

原載臺灣《秋水》詩刊137期，2008.04；臺灣《人間福
報》2008.05.26；安徽省文聯主管主辦，《安徽文學》
2010年.1-2期；北京市中國人民大學主辦《當代文萃》
2010.04期

Only the insects in the grass chirping by the ears

Restraining sad melody......

貓尾花

此刻綠光的湖岸仍隱蔽，

白夜漸次化開；

無樹的草坡裡沒有任何騷動，

不久，紫色的貓尾花將跟太陽同步說話。

《香港文學》2010.03；臺灣《乾坤》詩刊2010.04夏季號，
第54期

Cat-tail Daisy

Now the bank of the lake with green light still hiding

The white night gradually melting out

Treeless grass slope is quiet

Before long, purple cat-tail daisy will talk with the sun

流螢

穿出野上的蓬草

靈魂向縱谷的深處飛去

群峰之中

唯我是黑暗的光明

2009.05.22作

《香港文學》2010.03；臺灣《人間福報》2010.07.07

Twinkling Firefly

Through the clumps of grass of the field

My soul flies to the deep valley

Among the mountain peaks

Only me, bring the sunshine to the dark

秋暮

冬山河　鹹草鳴蛩

濱鷸　兩兩

惟有小水鴨

擾亂了整個水面

喚起白霧飛脫

留下溪口外

一片明霞

2009.05.22作

香港《香港文學》2010.03

Autumn Dusk

Dongshan river, salty herbs and crickets chirping

Dunlins, by twos and threes

Only the little teals

Disturbing the surface of the water

Arouse the white mist flying off

Leave a piece of bright rosy clouds

Outside the mouth of the brook

在那星星上

我望著花間雨露

像布穀鳥，掠過

潺潺的小河，而搖曳

在稻浪的，春之舞

2009.05.22作

《香港文學》2010.03刊登9首詩之一及插畫

Upon The Stars

I'm looking at the rain and dew among the flowers

Like cuckoo, passing by

The gurgling river, joggling along

Among the waves of the paddies, dance of the spring

夜祭
──紀念小林村夜祭而作

祂的目光被那歌不盡的牽曲
纏得如此淒迷，儘管供桌上什麼也沒有。
祂好像只有簡單的致詞，
簡單的致詞後便沒有笑容過。

離去的時候馱著族人的重載，
重載在這極小的舞圈中倦偎，
彷彿燃燒的每一種平埔語言的火，
圍繞著一群群小黑羊回家。

聽，那聲聲相疊　激蕩四山──

The Fete Of The Night

——For The Memory Of The Fete Of Night
At Xiaolin Village

His majesty's vision was twined by the long crooked notes

So miserable and fascinating,though nothing on the
credence

It seemed that he had only simple address

And no smile left after that

People left with heavy loading from the clansmen

which was snuggling around the tiny dancing circle

As if the burning fire on every kind of the Pingbu
language,

moving round the little black lamb on their way home

Listen,the voice echoes,vibrating the mountains
around

這裡沒有刀光劍影，

有的只是回頭再看一眼

在棧道上化為塵煙。

2009.08.16作〈紀念小林村〈88水災〉夜祭而作〉

附記：小林部落位於甲仙鄉東北方的小林村，1600多名村民有8成
　　　為平埔族西拉雅系大滿族人，守護神為番太祖、阿立祖或阿
　　　立母，供奉於公廨，每年農曆9月15日是部落「太祖夜祭」
　　　的日子。是平埔夜祭傳統祭儀的曲目之一，族人不分男女，
　　　不限人數，在太祖聖誕或開向夜祭時演出。

　　　台灣《文學台灣》季刊2009冬季號，第72期，此刊榮獲行政
　　　院文化建設委員會補助出版。

There are no the flashes and shadows of swords

Only left the looking back once more

That changed into smoke and dust on the road

木框上的盆花

你坐在石牆裡
用幾分之一秒的快門
捕捉日輪的俯臉
這或許是
你生命中僅有的一瞥。

山城之夜已緊緊收攏
裹住金絲雀顧憐倦藏的彩羽。
你在落雪裡
輕搖，無羈的空間
好似我未曾在你身旁——
是光融化了冰冷的書頁。

2010.02.19作
臺灣《笠》詩刊，第278期，2010.08.15

The Pot Flower In The Wooden Frame

You sit inside the stone wall

Shuttering in a fraction of a second

To catch the overlooking face of the sun

Perhaps

It's the only glimpse in your life

The night of the mountain town has closely furled

Swathed the colorful feather of the weary canary

You are in the falling snow

Slightly shaking,in the untamed space

As if I have never been by your side——

It is the light that melted the ice and cold of the page

傳說

我是風

詠嘆在牌樓南邊

靜穆地

在雲端深徑

一片雪清，留我

兩腳泥濘

是發光的落梅

是空蕩的鞦韆

朗讀著深埋的歷史

追問向奇萊山頂

而我堅持

以步移快遞寂寞

Legend

I am the wind

Chanting and singing by the southern archway

Solemnly

In the deep path of the clouds

An extensive clear snow,leave me

Bipod of mud

The flaring fallen plum

The unoccupied swing

Reciting the deeply buried history

Pursue the summit of Qilai Mount

I still persist

Fast deliver loneliness by moving my steps

蕭然

我邀柳杉一道啜茶

慢慢譜寫

一個褪了色的記憶

只有明月毫無顧忌地播撒

整個部落

2009.07.01作

臺灣《笠》詩刊，第274期，2009.12.15

Suddenly

I invite the Japan cedar for a cup of tea

Composing slowly

A faded memory

Only the bright moon spreading barbarically

The whole tribe

行經木棧道

黎明，帶著你折射出思想的芬芳來吧

跟著我，來吧，到石涼苔滑的棧道

在岩壁上像個僧侶披著雨帽

安謐中小青草比往年更茂更高

還帶著一切夢想沉睡的白蠟樹

冷杉和山毛櫸

用北方的民間歌謠

把夢想深藏在河流之心的夜空

來吧，把我也變一點兒

哪怕靈魂已凝成一座礁石

根根青草在波浪中起伏

2011.05.20作

台灣《創世紀》詩雜誌2011.09秋季號，第168期

Walk On The Wooden Plank Road

Dawn ,come with your fragrance reflecting your idea

Follow me,come to the plank road with cold rocks

  and slippery moss

On the rocky cliff like a monk wrapped around a rain hat

The tender grass in peace more luxuriant than the

  former years

Also along with the sound sleeping ash tree

Fir and Beech

With the northern folk ballad

Hiding the dream deeply in the dark night which is

  the heart of the river

Come along,and give me also a little change

Even if the soul has coagulated into a reef

Every grass tosses and rolls in the waves

早霧

窗臺外，遠處木犁

空蕩蕩地

單掛在田壟

那兒，山煙之上

你瞅著我，有好一陣

接著，我倚上沙發閉上眼睛

有如羊在霧中

想起了那年

瑟縮的二月

──透一股清冷

那是多久前的事兒了

我懷疑地問：

夜裡吹亂我頭髮的風

Morning Fog

Outside the window,the wooden plow beyond

Deserted

Hanging on the ribbing

There,upon the smoke of the mountain

You look at me,for rather a long time

Then,leaning on the sofa I close my eyes

As if a sheep in the fog

I remember that year

Curl up with cold in February

——go through a kind of pure cold

That was something long timer ago

I asked doubtfully:

The night wind blew and confused my hair

從上面經過　　回聲

落滿了河谷

過去的日子彷彿

一切都很重要

又都不很重要

就像早霧頑皮地溜走

說了等於沒說

2011.7.4作

香港《圓桌》詩刊，2011.10秋季號，第33期

From above ,echoing

Scattering upon the valley

The past days seemed

Everything is important

And also not very important.

Just like the morning fog gliding

What has said is like nothing has said

小雨

悄悄的回來了
似老僧入了定似的
閉目，一句也不說

偶爾
走在椅徑間彎著背
再停步，幾株薔薇竟熱望地開著
那一小撮的紅──
那是微笑的影子
掩映著她的臉 如波鱗般的光

轉瞬間
只剩老樹叢上的行雲

Drizzling

Come back quietly

Like an old monk in contemplation

Closed the eyes，no words to say

Occasionally

Walk on the pathway among the chairs with curved back

To stop again, a cluster of rosebush blooms enthusiastically

That pinch of red——

The shadow of a smile

Reflecting her face ,like the light of the waves

Transitorily

Only the floating clouds above the old bosks

低眉淺笑著，是小雨還是松風
老是吹我入兒時久遊的夢

2009.01.29作
原載臺灣《笠》詩刊，第271期，2009.06.15；轉載河北省
《詩選刊》2010.第4期

Smiling with the lowered eyebrow,

Is it the drizzling or the breeze

Always blowing me into my childhood dreams long

time ago

晚秋

在一片濃綠的陡坡
白光之下和風，把高地淅淅吹著。
你回首望，淡淡的長裙
弄散滿地丁香。

我看見
花瓣掉落山城垂楊
晨霧漸失。雲雀
驚動了松果，你淺淺一笑
彷彿世界揚起了一陣笙歌，
而笙歌在你的四周
有無法不感到讚嘆的奇趣。

Late Autumn

On a steep slope covering the dark green

Breeze in white light，rustling through the highland

You look back, in your long skirt of tint

Scattering cloves all over

I'v seen

Petals falling upon the drooping poplars in the mountain

  city

The fog disappearing . Skylarks

Startling the pinecones ,you smile faintly

As if a hail of Sheng music raising from the world

And it is around you

The amazing fantasy you cannot help to admire

今夜，

月已悄默，

只要用心端詳

石階草露也凝重

你離去的背影催我斷腸

就像秋葉搖搖欲墜

又怎抵擋得住急驟的風？

2009.03.14作

原載臺灣《秋水》詩刊，第143期，2009.10月

Tonight

The moon is silent

Only if you look carefully

The dew drops on grasses along the stone steps also
 dignified

The shadow of your back when you leave breaks my
 heart

Like autumn leaves tottering away

How can it stand the stormy wind?

在白色的夏季裡

白日變長

鐘錶習慣停在九點零一刻

在夜晚的寧靜中

我走向傳說

很久以前

玫瑰花的野坡上輕輕踱步

整個七月充滿憂鬱

靈魂是一座密林

風依然無休止地來

修復了我思想的安定

2011.5.22作
刊登臺灣《創世紀》詩雜誌2011.09秋季號，168期

In The White Summer

The days are getting longer

The clock used to stop at a quarter past nine

In the serenity of the night

I walk towards the legend

Long time ago

Gently strolling over the wild slope of roses

The whole July was gloomy

The soul is a dense forest

The wind was continuously blowing

Restoring the stability of my mind

牽引

午後　我的傷感

隨野麥嶺漫延

如浪往事

在彌留之際

雨同我打濕了時空

問你：為何時快時慢地緊跟著我

為何失望中的希望

總是一世羞澀

縱然萬頃碧波

誰能比崗哨不移的雲雨更重？

2011.5.21作

刊登臺灣《創世紀》詩雜誌2011.09秋季號，168期

Take You By The Hand

Afternoon ,my sorrow

Pervading through the mountain range of wild crops

Bygones like waves

At the moment of passing

Wetting the space with the rain

Ask you : Why do you follow me fast and slow

Why is the hope in the despair

Always shy all the time

Even if blue waves billowing

Who will be heavier than the clouds and rain that

　the sentry can't change

霧起的時候

我們不期而遇

原以為世上的一切都不孤寂

沒有客套寒暄

彷彿重逢是天經地義

然而

那熟悉的身影如晴雨

空漠地飄過在死亡中的廣場

霧正在升起

喧囂的人群　傘花晃動

街的盡頭　雨霧迷濛

空氣裡有著露珠的味道

一隻貓蜷縮在樹底

似乎等待著什麼

When The Fog Rises

We meet by chance

We used to believe nothing of the world is lonely

Without polite formula and conventional greetings

As if meeting again is perfectly natural

Nevertheless

That familiar figure like the rain with sunshine

Hollowly floating over the square of death

The fog is rising

Blatant Crowd and tossing flowers of umbrellas

At the end of the street misty rain and fog

Flavor of the dew in the air

A cat crouching under the tree

As if waiting for something

久雨初霽後
十月的黃昏　風淡描而過

2011.8.23作
刊登臺灣《創世紀》詩雜誌2011.12冬季號，169期

Newly fined after the long rain

Dusk in October ,breeze lightly drawing over

在蟲鳥唧唧鳴鳴的陽光裡

我們啜飲綠野
我們的鳳蝶沉溺風前
我們的豆娘啞然以對
那急竄的天牛已褪盡夏天

此外，四處儘是鳥語
那枯葉蝶　一派天真
以為時間　被攔截
在指甲花叢猛打呵欠

雲不曾改變其顏色
我們的思念也未見停歇

In The Sunshine With Chirping Crickets And Gurgling Birds

We sip and drink the green field

Our Papilios indulge in facing the wind

Our damselflies are mute to

That scurrying longicorn has already faded the summer

Besides, birds are singing all around

That Withered-leaf butterfly is so simple and puerile

It thinks that the time is hold up

Yawning among the clumps of camphires

Our yearning will not cease

As the cloud will never change its color

在柴塔尖山
與夜一起奔跑的季節

2010.10.16作
刊登臺灣《海星》詩刊，2011.08創刊號

On the mountain of firewood pinnacle of pagoda

The season we run with the night

附錄

概觀吳鈞《魯迅翻譯文學研究》書中的美學向度

◎林明理

摘要：

　　本論文主要以探討魯迅（註1）的翻譯文學為主，著重在對文本的分析及詮釋上，進而探討書中魯迅作品所呈顯的美學向度。魯迅作品中，常可窺見人性黑暗的一面，但直接提及美學問題的，實屬少見，卻是很值得關注的。

關鍵字：吳鈞，魯迅，翻譯文學，美學向度，詩

Overview Of The Aesthetic Dimension Of *A Study Of Lu Xun's Translated Literature* By Wu Jun

Abstract:

The main purpose of this article is to examine the texts and their interpretations,based on Lu Xun's translated literature,and to probe into the aesthetic dimension of Lu Xun's literature in the book.   From Lu Xun's works,it is more common for one to get a glimpse of the dark side of humanity than to talk about its aesthetic dimension which,however,is worthy of paying close attention to.

Keywords: Wu Jun,Lu Xun, Translated literature, Aesthetic
　　　　　dimension,poetry

一、前言

　　初讀這本書，給我的感覺是，吳鈞（註2）的創新意識是靈動、孜孜以求，刻苦鑽研中，由紛繁複雜到思理澄澈。深入細讀，我發現，吳鈞並非僅僅是勇於探索魯迅文學的那種對於新領域視野的開拓。其實，這是至今國內外罕見又出色的學術專著。看得出，魯迅的高妙文筆、思維博深，都足以讓吳鈞從中汲出哲思。在文獻的過濾和整合中，她努力地將對魯迅作品的感悟推向或衍生到翻譯理解的高度，並使自己站在了一個更高的起點。

　　魯迅一生共翻譯14個國家，近百位外國作家的200多種作品，字數達500萬之多。他曾說：「太偉大的變動，我們無力表現的，不過這也無須悲觀，我們既使不能表現他的全盤，我們可以表現他的一角。」（註3）文中第一章概論指出，魯迅是首先成為翻譯家，後來才成為文學家的。他能讀精深的日、德、英語，此外，還能讀俄羅斯文學，其最偉大的功績，是文學創作。在第六章裏，特別注重魯迅小說傳播對當代文學翻譯創作的成功經驗。雖說魯迅的文學翻譯和文學創作是緊密聯繫在一起的一個整體的兩個方面，然而，魯迅與文學翻譯方面的專門研究實為罕見。

最後，吳鈞有自己的結論。「魯迅文學翻譯和創新的世界傳播的成功證明：凡是具有生命力的文學藝術總是處在開放環境中的不斷學習、不斷更新自我的結果。」魯迅對翻譯文學的態度是嚴肅的、認真的。同樣的，魯迅對光明的憧憬和真理力量的堅信，才能使得他帶病，至55歲逝世前，始終頑強地固守著翻譯的陣地。魯迅也力求精細入微地體察原著精神，因而，從他筆端流出來的語言，就自然而然是傳神感人的。

從民族感情上講，魯迅一生之中，都在找尋一條出路，俯仰之間的所感所思，是探究國家民族的出路；他曾為五四文化新軍中最英勇的旗手。就個人而言，則是用文筆來反映現實人生。其所呈顯的思想對當代作家的啟示，多認為魯迅生動地描繪了中國人的習性、也能揭露和鞭撻他們身上的積陋、惰性和愚昧。

吳鈞指出，魯迅用他的文學翻譯和創作的手術刀觸到患者的傷痛深處，都是為了徹底地割除毒瘤。而這些生動

深刻的作品和創作描寫超越了膚淺的娛樂層次，進入人性的
深層審美層次。其藝術形象感人至深，這也是他民族憂患意
識的體現；他的獨創精神和精湛的翻譯藝術美，是當代世界
的學術思潮中不朽的文學典籍。在我看來，魯迅生命的意義
或許在回歸自然的原始感性力量中，由不斷升騰到永恆。

　　從理論發展的規律來說，魯迅的翻譯文學是借外國文
學來改造中國的國民性，改造中國的積弊社會。他認為翻
譯「首先的目的，就在於博覽外國的作品，不但移情，也
要益智。」（註4）我認為，魯迅文學思想的形成，是他繼
承中國文化傳統的基礎上，借鑑吸收西方先進哲學思想的
綜合結果；他將兩者融合起來，創造一種中西合璧的現代
文學。在魯迅翻譯故事裏，存有童話氣質中追求的人文關
懷，純粹而敏捷，幽默而堅毅，機智又詩意。在這裏，大
自然、充沛的藝術，引領著我們在哲人般的探索中，探尋
美學的力量。

　　中國的精神文化雖是抽象、虛構的，但卻是博大的、
深層次。而魯迅的翻譯文學響徹著時代的旋律，富有強烈
的感染力；其學習研究主要是為解決中國的實際問題。魯
迅認為翻譯是用來交流思想、振奮精神的。據此可知，他

想通過翻譯外國小說等作品，直面人生，達到他引進西方不同的哲學、藝術思維、與中國文化自然和諧交匯的高遠境界。在寫作態度上，他不僅擅於解剖他人、抨擊黑暗，而且更為嚴厲地剖析自我、超越自我。

　　總之，魯迅的翻譯是激發他本人創作激情和靈感的火種和源泉。在書內第二章裡，無疑，吳鈞也竭力排除自我主觀的論斷，完成著從魯迅精神層次到作品生成的轉譯和翻譯裏論家韋努蒂的比較研究，這正是此書最精采之處。這樣一來，她便使其研究視野有了新的實踐緯度。

　　文本第三章，吳鈞精闢地將魯迅翻譯文學歷史分為早期（1903-1908）、中期（1909-1926）、晚期（1927-1936）。其早期的翻譯手法以編譯、意譯為主；主要為科普作品和科學小說，代表作為法國儒勒·凡爾納（Jules Verne，1828-1905）的科學小說《地底旅行》。中期的翻譯手法轉向直譯，其代表譯作為長篇童話《小約翰》，在書中的第四章文本分析，有諸多獨到的分析研究。而魯迅晚期翻譯主要以蘇俄文學、美術史論和介紹西方版畫等為主；其中，最重要的譯作是俄國作家果戈理（Nicolai Vasilievich Gogol，1809-1852）《死魂靈》。

　　第五章中，探析魯迅的翻譯文學分類與藝術方法，將
魯迅直譯風格的奧妙和精彩處，為讀者的閱讀與研究提出
了新解。至此，吳鈞也給我們提供了一個繼續探索的文本
空間，引領著我們在探尋中直抵魯迅翻譯文學的美學向度
和詮釋，為本論文之研究成果。

二、魯迅對翻譯文學的貢獻

　　在魯迅深邃的思想裡，他善於把強烈的時代精神，同
鮮明多彩的藝術形象相融合，藉以直抒胸臆。筆者以為，
魯迅對翻譯文學的貢獻有三：

（一）對中國大時代精神的融聚

　　魯迅始終希望喚醒國人敢於正視自己的弱點，並吶喊
以覺悟並擺脫狹隘的愛國主義，在向西方先進國家的學習
中不斷增強自我，最終實現使中國自立於世界民族之林的
理想。在文本第二章裏，吳鈞提出魯迅與尼采有多災多難
的人生經歷和孤獨的心靈呼喚，使青年魯迅與尼采有著心

靈相通的一面。但魯迅對一生都被病痛和孤獨所折磨的天才尼采的理論是有選擇的接受的。

例如，魯迅並不贊成尼采的充滿懷疑主義和虛無主義的翻譯哲學。最可取的是，吳鈞提出魯迅與美國異化翻譯理論家韋努蒂的比較研究，魯迅所追求的譯文，並非一味仿效洋化，而是盡量保持原作的異域文化特色，以利文化的交流與瞭解，促進國民的覺醒。而美國勞倫斯‧韋努蒂（Lawren Venuti）則認為，在翻譯中譯者不必隱身，譯文中應當有譯者的身影。只有采取「異化」的翻譯，才能在譯文中保持原文的異國風情，這樣的翻譯才稱得上真正的譯文。

或許是隨著年齡的增長，閱歷的豐富，我感覺，書中有種靈動沉澱了越來越多的歲月的年輪和豐實感。魯迅在對嚴酷的社會現實冷靜觀察中，對悲傷與絕望的抗爭，常以現實主義的精神，來看待事物的發展和歷史的進步，以尋找個人生命的抗爭意義和價值。

（二）追求藝術形象、締造翻譯文學的意象美

早期魯迅文學翻譯文本分析中，基本上是採用直譯法，科學小說是他翻譯的一個重要內容。其中，吳鈞挑選

了《小約翰》為譯例中，探究魯迅翻譯的獨特風格；文本中，風景描寫譯筆優美傳神。比如「白的飛沫的邊鑲著海面，宛如黃鼬皮上，鑲了藍色的天鵝絨」。 還有「這有如漫長而夢幻地響著的琴聲，似乎繞繚著，然而是消歇的。」。（註5）這種意譯法顯示了魯迅豐富的想像力、增強了譯文的思想性，也使譯句更加富有詩意。記得意大利美學家克羅齊（Bendeto Croce）曾說：「感受的加工潤色，就是直覺」。顯然，魯迅的直覺即想像，是具有藝術思維性的靈感；其對色彩的想像也是一種匠心獨特的創造。又如「池邊是悶熱和死靜。大地因為白天的工作，顯得通紅而疲倦了。」（註6）魯迅的譯文總能引起我們更深刻的面對大自然，在其不斷突破的基點上，已獲得了高層次的創作藝術。

如果說魯迅早期的譯作在特有的幽默構思中，還透出銳利的麥芒；那麼，在他的晚期作品中，我們看到則是麥芒過後的金黃麥穗，在浪漫的哲思中流淌著舒緩的生命律動，滲透著抒情的、唯美的、獨特的藝術手法。這種氣韻蘊藉著濃鬱的美學意蘊，飽含著的質樸、純淨以及文字表達上的巧思，其舉重若輕的藝術形態構成了祥和幽雅、盎然生機的境界。

（三）在藝術手法上表現超逸與崇高熱烈的風格

吳鈞書中的文學氣韻還表現在對具有民族特色的懷舊意緒和尋求魯迅一生對譯作中質樸天趣的返歸情懷。魯迅晚年的譯文更體現出他所倡導的直譯風格，比如「主婦——她有血乳交融似的鮮活的臉色，美如上帝的晴天，她和柏拉圖諾夫就像兩個蛋，所不同的只是她沒有他那麼衰弱和昏沈，卻總是快活，愛說話。」（註7）這是何等的超凡！魯迅個人的憂患意識早已消融，升騰為以真樸、抒情為基調的意趣。我們讀到的意象是如此鮮活而特兀，又是這樣新穎而貼切的感覺。

我認為，第五章是全書最引人入勝的地方，也是一次從魯迅對真善美的不懈追求和譯作含義的深刻體現。在魯迅翻譯的第一階段，其中，詩歌翻譯意境優美、氣韻生動。比如翻譯莎士比亞的詩中「詩人的眼，在微妙的發狂的回旋，／瞥閃著，從天到地，從地到天；／而且提出未知的事物的形象來，作為想像的物體，／詩人的筆即賦與這些以定形，／並且對於空中的烏有，／則給以居處與名。」（註8）魯迅通過情境整體的想像，使詩譯獲得深遠綿長的美的極致；其情思淨純，有蘊含，給人以不同於別人的智慧與美融為一體之感。魯迅晚期譯作，透過返璞歸真、養性怡情的生活形態，無論是翻譯寫人、詠物、繪景或譯詩，在不假雕飾中呈現出譯文真淳的境界。

　　綜上所述，魯迅翻譯手法和藝術風格的豐富基調，在一定程度上延伸了吳鈞的研究深度，它們所留下的翻譯文學經驗，值得今後的研究工作者加以汲取。

三、魯迅翻譯文學的美學向度：苦難與甘美

　　魯迅在他的創作文學過程中，就試圖以翻譯的方式，完成中外文化的嫁接。他讀遍各國名詩文，繼承了中國文學優秀傳統，並深受西方現代主義詩歌的影響，成為「不斷更新藝術表現手法的高人」。

　　又何以魯迅人生的苦難能透過譯作而轉化為審美的愉悅？對此，筆者擬從以下兩個層面來說明：

（一）文學和翻譯中的審美觀照就是藝術

魯迅出生於浙江紹興一個逐漸沒落的士大夫家庭，時值中國多難之秋之際。可以想像，剛滿二十一歲的魯迅，見到國家受帝國列強的侵略、社會民不聊生這一切時，只有痛苦感，便有了以身許國的志向。他痛批中國幾千年來封建主義的精神毒瘤，遂而把民族革命和人民解放當成實踐理想的任務。魯迅的性格，絲毫不諂媚、屈奴。由於自幼受過詩書經傳的教育，對民間藝術、尤其是繪畫、研究歷史都有濃厚的興趣。所以，當他從外國文學思潮裏大量地吸收他所需要的材料，並轉而通過深沉的思想形成了翻譯文學的路綫，並蒸餾成藝術，化苦痛為美感。這就說明翻譯文學是魯迅生成美學向度的一種重要藝術力量，它處理其心靈最深處的悲哀與快樂。

（二）苦難與甘美的感情反應中所隱藏的真理

毛澤東曾讚譽說過，魯迅是偉大的思想家和偉大的革命家。魯迅在審悲與審美活動中，轉而將思考力集中對描寫苦難與愉悅的翻譯創作上；它具有強烈的吸引力，而使我們快樂地享受他創作中的自由與甜美。我所理解的是，魯迅之所以能從民族的苦難中，甚至醜陋的事物裡，發現美和詩意；這跟他翻譯文學時，常保持一份可貴的童心，就是保持自然賦予我們的真性相關。這樣就能領略、把握天地萬物之美，才能寫得真誠感人，才能自己主宰自己的心境，也展示了魯迅獨特的審美情趣和藝術追求。

　　然而，當我們翻開古今中外文學史，卻驚訝地發現，研究魯迅翻譯文學理論的叢書，屈指可數。這樣看來，我要喚醒讀者注意的是，值此社會風氣逐漸頹廢的關頭，在中國這兒，卻存有一筆無法估價的、迄今為止毋庸置疑的文學的財富。其中，隨著研究魯迅翻譯文學進程的逐步探索，在可以預見的將來，中國與外國文化的魯迅翻譯文學之比較研究，仍將成為既具有現代意義又具有學理深度的「顯學」。

　　吳鈞正是要在探索魯迅文學的時光隧道中，溫婉而執著地挽留住魯迅譯作時期過往的匆匆行跡。又或許吳鈞喜歡沉浸在對魯迅翻譯文學的追憶的不斷閃回，在懷古緬舊的感懷之中，讓我們重溫到魯迅當年的那種文思蘊藉與意蘊雋永。而吳鈞對待翻譯文學的研究態度，明顯也帶著魯

迅所要求要「一木一石疊起來」的意趣。書中敘述吸引人
之處，是超越藝術形象的更加深的美學向度。綜上所述，
魯迅的審美理想就是一道美的曙光，它直接貫穿醜陋的現
實與虛偽，而其翻譯文學的巧思及藝術魅力，也使讀者激
起愉悅之情。

　　我們要使這一研究具有實質性的歷史定位，就必須在
充分汲取相關的學術成果的同時，強化審美觀和審悲快感
的意識，在研究魯迅譯作與外國文學家比較的基礎上，應
拿出具有概括能力的研究模式。我認為，這是一本為學子
研究的魯迅翻譯文學作品集。如用心細讀過，也一定會在
其中得到某些教益。就會感到魯迅的譯作對我們的思想成
熟、能培養起潛移默化的作用。

2010年4月4日作
原載台灣佛光大學文學院歷史研究所　中國歷史學會編印《史
學集刊》年刊，第42期，2010.10
轉刊中國上海《上海魯迅研究》季刊，2011.07夏季號

註1. 周樹人〈1881-1936〉，筆名魯迅，浙江紹興人。是近代中國史上占據著重要地位的文學家、翻譯家、思想家；他的著作對於五四運動以後的中國文學產生深刻的影響。歷任北京大學講師、北京女子師範高等學校、廈門大學、廣州中山大學教授。

註2. 吳鈞〈1955-〉山東沽化人。文學博士，現任山東大學外語學院教授。

註3. 魯迅，《致賴少麒》，〈《魯迅全集》第13卷，人民文學出版社，2005年出版，第493頁〉。

註4. 魯迅，《「題未定」草》，《魯迅全集》第6卷，人民文學出版社2005年版，第364頁。

註5. 魯迅，《小約翰》，《魯迅譯文集》第4卷，人民文學出版社，1958年版，第64頁。

註6. 魯迅，《小約翰》，《魯迅譯文集》第4卷，人民文學出版社，1958年版，第23頁。

註7. 魯迅譯，《死魂靈》，《魯迅譯文集》第9卷，人民文學出版社，1959年版，第471頁。

註8. 魯迅譯，《苦悶的象徵》，《魯迅譯文集》，第3卷，人民文學出版社，1959年版，第36頁。

作者林明理文學作品目錄

作者林明理近五年文學作品目錄

（2007-2012春）

1. 南京《南京師範大學文學院學報》，2009年12月30日出版，
   總第56期。
2. 《安徽師範大學學報》，第38卷，第2期，總第169期，
   2010.03。
3. 江蘇省《鹽城師範學院學報》，第31卷，總第127期，
   2011.01。
4. 福建省《莆田學院學報》，第17卷，第6期，總第71期，
   2010.12。

5. 湖北省武漢市華中師範大學文學院主辦《世界文學評論》
   （集刊）／《外國文學研究》（AHCI期刊）榮譽出品，
   2011年05月，第一輯（總第11輯），頁76-78。

6. 山東省《青島大學學院學報》，第28卷，第2期，2011年6月。

7. 廣西大學文學院主辦《閱讀與寫作》，322期，2009.07。
   328期，2010.01、2011.07。

8. 西南大學中國新詩研究所主辦《中外詩歌研究》，2009第2
   期、2010第3期、2011第3期。

9. 江蘇省社會科學院主辦《世界華文文學論壇》、2009第4
   期、2010第3期、2011第2期。

10. 上海市《魯迅研究月刊》，2011夏，上海社會科學院出版社。

11. 北京中國人民大學主辦《當代文萃》，2010.04，發表詩2首。

12. 全國核心期刊山東省《時代文學》，2009第2、6、12期共3
    期封面推薦詩歌19首及詩評7篇。

13. 山東省作協主辦《新世紀文學選刊》2009.08、11、2009增
    刊，2010.01、03、2011增刊，發表詩歌28首及評論3篇。

14. 河北省作協主辦《詩選刊》2008.9、2009.07、2010.04，發
    表6首詩及詩評綠蒂1篇。

15. 新疆省優秀期刊《綠風》詩刊2009第3期、2010第3期，發表
    10首詩。

16. 遼寧省作協主辦《詩潮》詩刊，2009.12、2010.02、
    2011.02期封面底來訪合照照片之一（後排），發表詩4首
    及詩評綠蒂。

17. 香港《圓桌詩刊》，第26期，2009.09，發表詩評余光中1篇，詩2首。2011.09詩評1篇，第33期。

18. 香港《香港文學》，2010.03，發表9首詩、畫1幅。

19. 安徽省文聯主辦《安徽文學》，2010.02，發表詩2首。

20. 天津市作家協會主辦《天津文學》2009.12、2011.01，發表詩14首。

21. 北京《老年作家》，2009年第4期、2009.12、2011.01封面推薦、2011.02期發表書評.、2011.03期書評。

22. 大連市《網絡作品》、2010.第3期，發表詩歌4首。

23. 湖北省作協主辦《湖北作家》2009、秋季號，總第32期，發表書評古遠清教授1篇。

24. 中共巫山縣委宣傳部主辦《巫山》大型雙月刊，2010.02、2010.04，發表詩2首及畫作2幅。

25. 山東省蘇東坡詩書畫院主辦《超然詩書畫》，總第1、第9期，發表詩畫，《超然》詩刊，總第12期2009.12、13期2010.06、15期2011.06，發表詩17首。2011.12刊登書畫及評論1篇。

26. 美國《poems of the world》季刊，2010-2011秋季，發表譯詩9首。

27. 中國《黃河詩報》，總第5期，發表詩3首。

28. 山東省《魯西詩人》，2009.05，發表詩4首。

29. 福州《台港文學選刊》，2008.09發表詩5首，2009發表詩歌。

30. 美國《亞特蘭大新聞》，2010.02-2011.07發表8篇評論及詩1首。

31. 美國《新大陸》雙月詩刊，任名譽編委，2009第110期迄127期發表詩34首。詩評2篇。

32. 《中國微型詩萃》第二卷，香港天馬出版，2008.11，及《中國微型詩》25首。

33. 臺灣《國家圖書館館訊》特載，2009.11發表書評1篇。

34. 臺灣「國圖」刊物，《全國新書資訊月刊》2010.03起至2011.12，第135、136、137、138、140、142、143、144、146、147、148、149、150、151、152、153、155、156期，發表詩評及書評共17篇。

35. 臺灣《創世紀》詩雜誌，160-169期（至2012春季，發表詩14首，及詩評14篇）。

36. 臺灣《文訊》雜誌，2010.1、3、7、12、2011.08、2012.02（發表評論6篇）。

37. 臺灣《笠》詩刊，2008起，第263-287期（至2012.02止詩發表42首及詩評10篇）。

38. 臺灣中國文藝協會《文學人》季刊，2010-2011，發表詩7首及評論2篇。

39. 臺灣《文學臺灣》，第72-78期（至2011秋季），發表詩8首。

40. 臺灣《新原人》，2010夏季號，發表詩2首。

41. 臺灣佛光大學文學院中國歷史學會《史學集刊》，第42集2010.10，發表書評〈概觀吳鈞《魯迅翻譯文學研究》有感〉。

42. 臺北市保安宮主辦，《大道季刊》2011.01，發表古蹟旅游論述。

43. 臺灣《乾坤》詩刊，2010-2011.冬季，第50-60期，發表詩33首及詩評8篇。

44. 臺灣《秋水》詩刊，2008-2012.01止，發表詩21首及詩評3篇，第137-151期。

45. 臺灣《人間福報》副刊，詩2008-2011.11止，刊登詩56首、散文小品等32篇。

46. 臺灣高雄市《新文壇》季刊，至2011冬季，發表詩22首及詩畫評論7篇。

47. 臺灣《海星》創刊號，至2011.11冬季第2期止發表詩5首，詩評1篇。

48. 山東省作協主辦《新世紀文學選刊》，2009年擔任刊物的封面水彩畫家一年，獲其主辦文學筆會「詩歌一等獎」證書。2009.08至2010.03共發表詩28首，詩評3篇。

49. 遼寧省作協《中國詩人》2011.05卷刊登林明理評白長鴻詩評1文。

50. 重慶市《世界詩人》季刊（混語版）總第64期，2011.冬季號，詩評1篇。

51. 2011.10.14應邀台灣高雄應用科技大學人文學院丁旭輝院長邀請至校任新詩組三位評審之一。評文收錄成書。

52. 臺灣《新地》，第16期，2011冬季號，刊登詩2首。

53. 河南省《商丘師範學院學報》2012年第1期，刊登書評丁旭輝一篇。

54. 2011.12.08應邀於高應大人文學院丁旭輝院長至校擔任「佛文杯」評審，撰寫一文，刊登《臺灣時報》2011.12.16，頁18。

55. 臺灣真理大學臺灣文學資料館發行《臺灣文學評論》2011年10月，第11卷第4期。刊登書評莫渝

56. 臺灣佛光大學文學院中國歷史學會《史學集刊》，第43集，2011.11，發表書評蔡振輝。

57. 《鹽分地帶文學》2011.12，刊登一詩。

譯者吳鈞教授作品目錄

學術專著monograph

1. 《魯迅翻譯文學研究》，齊魯書社，2009
   monograph：WU Jun,*Study of Lu Xun's Translated Literature*,Qilu Press,Jinan,2009

2. 專著：《學思錄──英語教研文集》，內蒙古人民出版社，
   1999
   monograph: WU Jun,*Learning and Thinking —A Collection of Wu Jun' Papers on English Teaching and Research*,Inner Mongolia People's Press,Hohhot,1999

學術論文academic theses

1. 吳鈞，〈論魯迅詩歌翻譯與世界傳播〉，《山東社會科學》，2011.11
   WU Jun,"On The Translation Of Lu Xun's Poems And Its World Communication",*Shandong Social Science* ,11,2011
2. 吳鈞，〈易經英譯與世界傳播〉，《周易研究》，第1期，2011
   WU Jun,"On The Translation And Communication Of Yi Jing ",*Studies Of Zhouyi*,1,2011
3. 吳鈞，〈魯迅『中間物』思想的傳統文化底蘊〉，《周易研究》，第1期，2008
   WU Jun,"The Traditional Cultural Deposits In LU Xun's Idea Of 'Intermediate Object'",*Studies Of Zhouyi*,1,2008

4. 吳鈞，〈魯迅『中間物』思想的傳統文化血脈〉，《齊魯學刊》，第2期，2008

    WU Jun,"On the Heritage of Chinese Tradition of LU Xun's Idea of 'Intermediate Object'",*Qilu Journal*,2,2008

5. 吳鈞，〈論魯迅的憂患意識〉，《西北師大學報》，第6期，2007

    WU Jun,"On Lu Xun's Consciousness of Suffering",*Journal of Northwest Normal University (Social Sciences)*,44(6),2007

6. 吳鈞，〈從儒家思想看魯迅精神與中國文化傳承〉《甘肅社會科學》第4期，2007

    WU Jun,"On LU Xun's Spirits and the Succession of Chinese Culture from the Perspective of the Confucianism",*Gansu Social Sciences*,4,2007

7. 吳鈞，〈從《周易》看魯迅精神與民族魂〉，《周易研究》，第2期，2007

    WU Jun," On LU Xun's Spirits and Chinese National Soul from the Perspective of *Zhouyi*",*Studies Of Zhouyi*,2,2007

8. 吳鈞，〈略論《苔絲》創作手法的悲劇意味〉，《齊魯學刊》，第9期，2002

    WU Jun,"On the Tragical Significance of Thomas Hardy's Literary Creation of Tess of the D' Urbervilles",Qilu Journal,5,2002

9. 吳鈞，〈從《周易》的原點看人文精神與新世紀跨文化交際〉，《周易研究》，第6期，2002

   WU Jun,"A Study of Humanism and Intercultural Communication of the New Century from the Origin of Zhouyi",Studies Of Zhouyi,3,2002

10. 吳鈞，〈略論《苔絲》的當代啟示性〉，《東岳論叢》，第9期，2002

    WU Jun,"Talk On the Contemporary Significance of the Tragedy of Tess",*Dongyue Tribune*,23(5),2002

11. 吳鈞，〈童話王國民俗見聞〉，《民俗研究》，2002

    WU Jun," Folk-customs of Denmark,the Kingdom of Fairy Tales",*Folklore Studies*,3,2002

12. 吳鈞，〈論《紫色》的思想藝術性〉，《齊魯學刊》，第3期，2005

    WU Jun,"On the Ideas and Art of *the Color Purple*",*Qilu Journal*,3,2005

13. 吳鈞，〈艾米莉‧狄更生詩歌創作特徵與藝術手法〉，《臨沂師範學院學報》，第10期，2002

    WU Jun,"Emily Dickinson's Creative Characteristics and Artistic Skills in Her Poems",*Journal Of Linyi Teachers' University*,10,2002

14. 吳鈞，〈非專業研究生英語教學中的方法探討〉，《山東外語教學》，第6期，2002

    WU Jun,"Discussion on the English Teaching Methods for Graduate Students of Non-English Majors",*Shandong Foreign Languages Journal*,6,2002

15. 吳鈞，〈略論菲茨杰拉德的創作思想、藝術手法及現實意義〉，《河西學院學報》，第6期，2002

    WU Jun,"A Brief Discussion of F. S. Fitzgerald's Creative Thinking,Ways of Artistic Expression and their Significance",*Journal of Hexi University*,6,2002

16. 吳鈞，〈憂鬱的藍玫瑰〉，《萊陽農學院學報》，第5期，2002

    WU Jun,"Melancholy Blue Rose",*Journal of Laiyang Agricultural College (Social Science Edition)*,5,2002

17. 吳鈞，〈從《雷雨》創作的悲劇女性形象看經典文學的傳播〉，《山東文學》，第9期，2006

    WU Jun,"From the Creation of the Characters of the Tragic Women in the Play *Thunderstorm* to See the Communication of Classical Literature",*Shandong Literature*,9,2006

18. 吳鈞，〈從中西電影中的女性形象塑造談起〉，《華夏文壇》，第12期，2005

    WU Jun,"A Discussion of the Creation of the Characters of Women in Chinese and Western Movies",*China Literary World*,12,2005

19. 吳鈞，〈從影視人物形象塑造看中西文化歷史發展〉，《山東文學》，第6期，2005

WU Jun,"From the Creation of Characters on TV and Screen to See the Culture from the East and the West",*Shandong Literature*,6,2005

20. 吳鈞，〈從電影中的女性形象塑造看全球化語境下的跨文化交際〉，《時代文學》，第6期，2005

WU Jun,"Talk on Cross-culture Communication from the angle of the Creation of the Characters of Women in Movies",*Literature of the Times*,6,2005

21. 吳鈞，〈愛倫·坡詩歌創作風格〉，《中外詩歌研究》，第2期，2003

WU Jun,"The Style of Edgar Allan Poe's Poetry",*Chinese and Foreign Poetics*,2,2003

22. 吳鈞，〈英語顏色詞的翻譯與跨文化交際〉，《現代文秘》，第2期，2002

WU Jun,"The Translation of the Words of Colors and the Cross-culture Communication",*Modern Secretarial*,2,2002

23. 吳鈞，〈英語實物顏色詞的構成及修辭作用〉，《寧波大學學報》，第4期，1995

WU Jun,"Some New Ideas on the Formation and the Rhetorical Functions of the Color Words from Substances in English,*Journal of Ningbo University*,4,1995

24. 吳鈞，〈外貿英語談判課中的模擬法運用新探〉，《寧波大學學報》，第2期，1996

   WU Jun,"Some New Ideas on the Class of Simulation of Foreign Trade Negotiation",*Journal of Ningbo University*,2,1996

25. 吳鈞，〈模擬教學法在外貿英語談判課中的運用〉，《山東外語教學》，第3期，1996

   WU Jun,"Simulation Teaching Applied in the Class of Foreign Trade Negotiation",*Journal of Shandong Foreign Languages Teaching*,3,1996

26. 吳鈞，〈多彩的道路，曲折的道路──從愛麗絲・沃克的《紫色》看美國婦女的自救道路〉，《學習與思考》，第4期，1996

   WU Jun,"A Colorful and Devious Road—an Observation of American women's Self-saving by Way of the Novel *the Color Purple*",*Learning and Thinking*,4,1996

27. 吳鈞，〈顏色的象徵──從一部小說看美國婦女的自救道路〉，《現代化》，第6期，1996

   WU Jun,"The Symbolic Meaning of Colors—from one Novel to See American Women's Road of Self-saving",*Modernization*,6,1996

28. 吳鈞，〈從《了不起的蓋茨比》看金錢夢的破滅〉，《學習與思考》，第9期，1995

   WU Jun,"From the Novel *Great Gatsby* to See the Break of the Dream of Gold",Learning and Thinking,9,1995

Journals like Studies of Zhouyi,Qilu Academic Study,Journal of Northwest Normal University (Social Sciences) and Gansu Social Sciences are indexed in Chinese Social Science Citation Index (CSSCI)

翻譯translation

1. 翻譯吳開晉詩歌〈寫在海瑞墓前〉、〈致瀑布〉和〈灘江〉，《老年作家》，第4期，2009
   "In Front of the Tumulus Of Hairui","To Waterfall" and "Li River",*Elderly Writers*,4,2009,Poet: WU Kaijin,Translator: WU Jun

2. 翻譯吳開晉詩歌〈椰林歌聲〉，香港大型漢英雙語詩學季刊《當代詩壇》，第51-52期，2009
   "Songs in the Coconut Wood",*Contemporary Poetry*,51-52,2009,Poet: WU Kaijin,Translator: WU Jun

3. 翻譯吳開晉詩歌〈久違的雷電〉，《當代詩壇》，第51-52期，2009
   "The Long Absent Thunder and Lighting",*Contemporary Poetry,*51-52,2009,Poet: WU Kaijin,Translator: WU Jun

4. 翻譯《中國沾化吳氏族譜》序言，中國檔案出版社，2008
   Preface of *Pedigree of Wu Family Zhuanhua*,China Archives Press,Beijing,2008,Translator: WU Jun

5. 翻譯吳開豫著《自珍集》，中國文史出版社，2006
   Collection of the Poems which I cherish,China Literature and History Publishing House,Beijing,2006,Writer: WU Kaiyu,Translator: WU Jun

6. 翻譯〈易理詮釋與哲學創造〉，《周易研究》（增刊），2003
   "Philosophical Creation and Interpretation by Yi Principles",*Study of Zhouyi,supplement,*2003,Writer: GAO Ruiquan,Translator: ZHANG Wenzhi,WU Jun

7. 編譯《老屋的倒塌──埃德加・愛倫坡驚險故事》，山東文藝出版社，2000
   The Fall of the House of Usher── The New Edition of Edgar Allan Poe's Adventurous Stories,Shandong Literature and Arts Press,Jinan,2000,Translator: WU Jun

8. 翻譯吳開晉教授詩歌〈土地的記憶〉，1996，榮獲世界詩人大會（東京）詩歌和平獎
   "The Memory of the Land",1996,Poet: WU Kaijin,Translator: WU Jun

This translated poem won the Peace Prize in World Congresses of Poets for the celebration of the 60th Anniversary of the Victories in the Global Anti-fascist 1996 (Tokyo).

9. 漢譯英：林明理詩歌漢譯英臺灣林明理詩歌〈雨夜〉、〈夏荷〉，《*World Poetry Anthology 2010* 》（2010 第三十屆世界詩人大會世界詩選）臺灣，328-331頁

Translation of Chinese poem to English:"Rainy Night","Summer Lotus"by Lin Mingli，World Poetry Anthology 2010，p.328-331

10. 漢譯英：林明理詩歌〈夏蓮〉，發表於美國《世界詩歌》，第14-4期2010

Translation of Chinese poem to English:"Summer Lotus"by Lin Mingli，*Poems Of The World,USA*,Volume 14 -4,2010

文學創作Literary Creation

詩歌創作

1. 詩歌：〈吳鈞悉尼詩歌選12首〉，《華夏文壇》2010年第三期
Poems:"12 Poems In Sydney by Wu Jun",*China Literary World*,3,2010

2. 詩歌：〈悉尼隨感錄11首〉，《彼岸》2011年第三期
   Poems: "Free Ideas Of Sydney" (11 Poems by Wu Jun) , *On The Other Shore* 3,2011

3. 詩歌：《時光的葉片》(〈路〉、〈夏之偶感〉、〈總是〉、〈淡淡的心湖〉)，網路作品，第1期，2010年
   Poems: *The Leaves of the Time* ("Road", "Summer Inspiration By Chance" , " Always","Slightly Waved Lake Of Heart") ,Network Literature,1,2010

4. 詩歌：〈天望〉、〈家鄉的國槐〉、〈母親〉，《山東文學》，2010.7
   Poems: "Looking at the Heaven","Sophora Tree Of My Homeland" , "Mother", *Shandong Literature*, 2010.7

散文創作

1. 散文：〈塞外江南張掖游〉，《華夏文壇》，2011-11
   Prose:"My Travele To Zhangye ,The 'Jiangnan'Of The North Of The Great Wall",*China Literary World*,11.2011

2. 散文〈父愛如山〉，《華夏文壇》，第3期，2009
   Prose:"Mountains of Love of My Father",*China Literary World*,3,2009

3. 散文〈槐香如故〉，《當代小說》，第10期，2007
   Prose:"The Fragrance of Sophora Tree of My Hometown", *Contemporary fiction*,10,2007

4. 散文〈魯橋眺望〉，《華夏文壇》，第4期，2007
   Prose:"A View from the Bridge of Lu",*China Literary World*,4,2007

後記

　　本書大多是我5年來從事詩歌創作的一個結集。出版前得到了山東大學尊敬的吳開晉教授（吳鈞教授的叔父）惠贈題字、名評家古遠清教授惠賜序言，以及現任外語系吳鈞教授特別協助翻譯了全書共66首新詩，特此致謝。此外，也感謝臺灣「國家圖書館」前館長顧敏教授、現任「國圖」館長曾淑賢博士、佛光大學范純武教授、文津出版丘鎮京教授、佛光大學蔡秉衡教授、成功大學陳昌明教授、高應大丁旭輝院長、林秀蓉博士、台文館館長李瑞騰教授、副館長張忠進老師、萬卷樓出版陳滿銘教授們等師友的鼓勵。特別是向吳英美主編、曾坤賢主任、認真善良的鄭雅云編校致上最深的謝意；因為有雅云的支持與打氣，讓筆者有不斷成長的機會於這片詩壇沃土。並感謝海內外各刊物主編張默、辛牧、方明、封德屏、杜秀卿、莫渝、郭楓、林煥彰、莫云、楊濤、彭瑞金、《世界詩人》張智博士、林佛兒、李若鶯、塗靜怡、陶然、潘琼來、季宇、秀實、秀珊、曲近、郁蔥、張映勤、《Poems of the World》Dr.Elma.、李牧翰、李浩、羅繼仁、白長鴻、陳銘華、許月芳、周慧珠、劉大勇、謝明洲、柳笛，及南京師範大學吳錦教授、鹽城師院郭錫健教授、青島大學田軍教授、莆田學院彭文宇教授、華中師範大學鄒建軍教授、安徽師範大學王世華教授、鹽城師院陳義海教授、郭錫健教授、商丘師範學院高建立教授、重慶師範大學黃中模教授、吳思敬教授、傅天虹教授、王柯教授、莊偉傑教授、山東大學孫基林教授等教授的支持。也感謝鍾鼎文老師、非馬博士、辛鬱、魯蛟、綠蒂理事長、鄭烱明、曾貴海、羊子喬、許達然教授、丁文智、廖俊穆、鄭烱明、藍雲、周伯乃、吳德亮、黃騰輝、周玉山博士、楊允達博士、許其正、喬林、鄭琇月醫師、沈明福醫師、佛光美術館館長如常法師、副館長妙仲法師、徐錦成老師等詩友的愛護。最後謹向秀威資訊發行人宋政坤先生、副總編蔡登山及責任編輯孫偉迪、圖文排版楊尚蓁、封面設計陳佩蓉為本書所付出的辛勞致意。

2011年12月12日　林明理

語言文學類　PG0698

回憶的沙漏
——中英對照詩集

作　　者／林明理
譯　　者／吳　鈞
主　　編／蔡登山
責任編輯／孫偉迪
圖文排版／楊尚蓁
封面設計／陳佩蓉
封面繪圖／林明理

發 行 人／宋政坤
法律顧問／毛國樑　律師
印製出版／秀威資訊科技股份有限公司
　　　　　114台北市內湖區瑞光路76巷65號1樓
　　　　　電話：+886-2-2796-3638　傳真：+886-2-2796-1377
　　　　　http://www.showwe.com.tw
劃撥帳號／19563868　戶名：秀威資訊科技股份有限公司
　　　　　讀者服務信箱：service@showwe.com.tw
展售門市／國家書店（松江門市）
　　　　　104台北市中山區松江路209號1樓
　　　　　電話：+886-2-2518-0207　傳真：+886-2-2518-0778
網路訂購／秀威網路書店：http://www.bodbooks.com.tw
　　　　　國家網路書店：http://www.govbooks.com.tw
圖書經銷／紅螞蟻圖書有限公司
　　　　　114台北市內湖區舊宗路二段121巷28、32號4樓
　　　　　電話：+886-2-2795-3656　傳真：+886-2-2795-4100

2012年2月BOD一版
定價：340元
版權所有　翻印必究
本書如有缺頁、破損或裝訂錯誤，請寄回更換

國家圖書館出版品預行編目

回憶的沙漏：中英對照詩集 / 林明理著；吳鈞譯. -- 一
版. -- 臺北市：秀威資訊科技,2012.02
　　面；　公分. -- (語言文學類；PG0698)
　BOD版
　中英對照
　ISBN 978-986-221-900-3(平裝)

851.486　　　　　　　　　　　　　　100027177

讀 者 回 函 卡

感謝您購買本書，為提升服務品質，請填妥以下資料，將讀者回函卡直接寄回或傳真本公司，收到您的寶貴意見後，我們會收藏記錄及檢討，謝謝！
如您需要了解本公司最新出版書目、購書優惠或企劃活動，歡迎您上網查詢或下載相關資料：http:// www.showwe.com.tw

您購買的書名：_____

出生日期：_____年_____月_____日

學歷：□高中 (含) 以下　　□大專　　□研究所 (含) 以上

職業：□製造業　□金融業　□資訊業　□軍警　□傳播業　□自由業
　　　□服務業　□公務員　□教職　　□學生　□家管　□其它____

購書地點：□網路書店　□實體書店　□書展　□郵購　□贈閱　□其他

您從何得知本書的消息？

　□網路書店　□實體書店　□網路搜尋　□電子報　□書訊　□雜誌
　□傳播媒體　□親友推薦　□網站推薦　□部落格　□其他_____

您對本書的評價：(請填代號　1.非常滿意　2.滿意　3.尚可　4.再改進)

　封面設計____　版面編排____　內容____　文／譯筆____　價格____

讀完書後您覺得：

　□很有收穫　□有收穫　□收穫不多　□沒收穫

對我們的建議：_____

_____

_____

_____

11466
台北市內湖區瑞光路 76 巷 65 號 1 樓

秀威資訊科技股份有限公司　　　收
　　　　　BOD 數位出版事業部

....

（請沿線對折寄回，謝謝！）

姓　　名：＿＿＿＿＿＿＿＿　年齡：＿＿＿＿　性別：□女　□男

郵遞區號：□□□□□

地　　址：＿＿＿＿＿＿＿＿＿＿＿＿＿＿＿＿＿＿＿＿＿＿

聯絡電話：(日) ＿＿＿＿＿＿＿＿＿＿　(夜) ＿＿＿＿＿＿＿＿＿＿

E-mail：＿＿＿＿＿＿＿＿＿＿＿＿＿＿＿＿＿＿＿＿＿＿